AVARITIA

SHADES OF SIN

AVARITIA

COLETTE RHODES

TO THE AIRBNB HOST WHO SAID "BUT YOU LOOK LIKE SUCH A SWEET LADY!" WHEN I TOLD HER WHAT I WAS WORKING ON.

AVARITIA IS A MONSTER ROMANCE BETWEEN A HUMAN AND HER NOT-QUITE-HUMAN PARTNER, SUITABLE FOR READERS OVER 18.

CW: SEXUAL CONTENT, TENTACLE PLAY, PRIMAL PLAY, SOMNOPHILIA.

"BETWEEN TWO EVILS, I ALWAYS PICK THE ONE I NEVER TRIED BEFORE."

- MAE WEST

PROLOGUE

TEN YEARS EARLIER

So, how was your Criminal Law class? I feel like of all the classes you're taking, that one sounds the most interesting," I said to my boyfriend, tucking my phone between my ear and shoulder as I moved the pot of rice off the heat to finish cooking.

"Well, obviously, it's interesting, but it's not like a crime show like you're probably imagining, Eri," Sebastian replied dismissively. *"It's a really complex topic."*

"Right." I cringed at my own ignorance. "Sorry. I didn't mean for it to come out like that."

Sebastian was a nice guy. The best guy. *Everyone* said so. He clearly didn't *mean* to make me feel like an idiot whenever I tried to talk about what he was doing at law school. It was an accident. Besides, I could have looked into it more, figured out what it was he was actually studying.

I was just on edge from him being so far away, that was all. Long-distance relationships were challenging for anyone. Once Sebastian graduated and moved back home, and once we weren't four hundred and forty-eight miles apart, things would be back to normal. Everything would be wonderful again. He'd either find a job at a regular law firm here or work for the Hunters Council's in-house legal team. I'd be a manager at Furocious by then, and we'd finally have that winter wonderland wedding we'd always talked about.

Just two and three-quarter years to go.

"*Mom says you haven't visited her in a while,*" Sebastian said in a faintly accusatory tone, drawing me back to the unpleasantness of the present rather than the daydreams I preferred spending my time in.

"Work has been super busy—" I began, wincing slightly at the reminder that I was overdue to go kiss the ring at my future mother-in-law's house. Sebastian was *everything*, and of course I loved him more than life, but he was a teensy bit of a mama's boy. But it was fine. He'd probably grow out of it once we were married and had kids of our own.

As he regularly pointed out, I didn't have a good idea of what a normal parental relationship looked like, so I couldn't judge his.

"*It's a pet store, Eri. You're not curing cancer.*"

"No, I know that—"

"*And you know how hard it's been on Mom with me deciding to go out of state for law school. It's always been us against the world, and she's really struggling. I'm really counting on you to help her out, Eri. Maybe drop a meal over there or something. Wifey shit, you know. I don't trust anyone else to do it.*"

A small flutter of hopeful butterflies took flight at the word *wifey*. "She doesn't like my cooking."

"*You could make something she likes. You don't have to put spices in everything. She also wants to know what time you're picking her up to come and visit me this weekend?*"

Shit.

"I, um, thought this weekend was just going to be the two of us?" *Silence.* "It's just that it's our anniversary, and we were going to do something special," I tacked on hurriedly. He'd probably forgotten.

I mean, it wasn't *great* that he'd forgotten our five-year anniversary, but he was busy. Law school was hard. I shouldn't judge.

"*I'm all she has, Eri.*"

And there it was. The argument I couldn't win. The fight I could never have because I'd look like the devil incarnate if I said anything to counter that.

It felt like swallowing bile to concede defeat, but I forced it down anyway. "Maybe we could do something for our anniversary next time I'm down. Just the two of us."

Sebastian exhaled. "*I knew you'd understand. You're the fucking best. You'll sort out the logistics with Mom for this weekend, yeah? I'm due at a study session.*"

"Absolutely, of course. You should go." I took a steadying breath, trying to find some sense of inner calm. Sebastian was busy. Law school was a lot of pressure, and Deb's constant whining about him moving away wasn't helping. He needed me. I didn't want to add to the already huge load he was carrying.

"I love you," I added, hoping my voice sounded cheerier than I felt. I hated this feeling of constantly counting down, waiting for the good times to start, never being able to enjoy the present. My whole life was on hold, and while I'd voluntarily agreed to this arrangement, I couldn't help but resent it a little at times too.

And that only made my self-loathing worse. As Sebastian often pointed out, I was the one with everything to gain from this temporary pain. He'd make good money once he graduated, and he was doing it for *us*.

"*Love you,*" Sebastian replied easily, the words providing a familiar sense of comfort after years of hearing them. "*I'll talk to you tomorrow.*"

I swallowed thickly. "Yeah. I'll talk to you tomorrow."

By the time the end of my shift rolled around on Friday evening, I was the closest I'd ever been to bailing on a visit to see Sebastian. I wouldn't, of course, but I *really* felt like it.

A delayed delivery meant that Mrs. Hartford couldn't buy Rembrandt's usual brand of kibble, causing her to have a complete meltdown in the middle of the store. Just when I'd calmed her down, a new customer arrived with an adorable little spoodle pup, who'd promptly peed on my canvas sneakers.

I'd had better days at work.

My phone rang through the car speakers, interrupting the big booty anthem I'd been bopping along to and making me jump.

"Hello?" I said, accepting the call without taking my eyes off the road to check the caller. Or rather, assuming it was Sebastian, because no one else ever called me.

"*V.*" Nope, not Sebastian. It was one of my roommates, Da-Eun, who'd *never* called me.

"Everything okay?" *Please don't say there's a gas leak. I can't take another thing going wrong today.*

She whispered something too low for me to catch, and I stabbed the volume button a few times. "Can you repeat that? I didn't catch it—"

"*I said that your boyfriend's mom is here. She said you were supposed to pick her up two hours ago or something? But you never showed?*"

"I was supposed to pick her up at six," I gritted out, which was still half an hour away. Just enough time for me to get home, change, scrub the pee-foot, and grab my bag before driving until one a.m.

"*I'm not getting into it,*" she replied. I couldn't be mad about that. My roommates and I were passing acquaintances at best, and it's not like Deb was the politest of house guests. My roomies were also one-hundred-percent human, so I couldn't mention the fact that Deb was not only my boyfriend's mom but my superior in a secret monster-killing organization. I had 99 problems and Deb was all of them. "*I'm just telling you that she's here and she's waiting in your room.*"

"In my *room*?!"

"I did try to suggest she wait in the living room, but she's kind of terrifying for a five-foot-nothing suburban soccer mom."

"I appreciate the effort, thanks," I replied weakly, already reaching for the *end call* button and stepping a little harder on the gas. *Don't crash Sebastian's car, he'll be so pissed.* "I'll be there in five, okay? Thanks for the heads-up."

Shit, shit, shit.

Deb was probably just sitting on the edge of my bed, quietly fuming. Right? Right. She wouldn't snoop.

I mean, she'd never showcased any understanding of boundaries before, but it was probably in there somewhere, buried under layers of hostility. So long as she wasn't looking through anything, there was nothing to worry about except hours of miserable car chat.

Besides, I'd put everything away carefully last night, hadn't I? Of course I had. I was always careful. What I was doing was wrong; I didn't take any unnecessary risks with it.

I parked in my usual spot a little up the street, my tote bag snagging on the hand brake as I half fell out of the car in a rush.

"Fuck, fuck, come on," I mumbled to myself, yanking the strap free and slamming the door behind me before booking it down the street, my drink bottle banging uncomfortably against my hip as I shouldered the bag. I was panting with exertion by the time I got to the front door, and Da-Eun kindly opened it for me after twenty seconds of me fumbling around in my pockets, looking for my keys.

"Good luck," she muttered, flopping down on the couch and pressing her phone nearly to her nose.

"Thanks," I panted, skidding slightly on the greige floorboards as I rounded the corner and headed down the hallway to my room.

Positive thinking. Positive thinking. She's just sitting on the edge of your bed, scowling at you in disdain, acting like you're the one who got the time wrong. Apologize profusely for having the gall to be at work, usher her out to the car, and drive to Albuquerque in silence with a pee-soaked sneaker. Easy. Nothing to stress about. It's going to be fine.

It was not fine.

I pushed open the not-quite-closed door to my pastel pink bedroom, finding precisely what I'd hoped to avoid. I was pretty sure I'd had a nightmare about this exact scenario once after I'd eaten too much cheese at dinner.

At least she'd only found half my stash.

"What. Is. This?" Deb asked, her usually pale face flushed crimson with outrage.

I opened my mouth, hoping that some kind of logical, acceptable explanation would magic its way out of my brain, but eventually gave up and closed it again, quickly shutting the door behind me so my roommates didn't overhear this horror show in progress.

"I know it looks bad—"

"You are a *Hunter*," Deb hissed, thankfully keeping her voice down. "Have you forgotten that? You are meant to *rid* our world of the creatures of the night. And all along, you're hiding this, this *disgusting* hoard? It's... it's *depraved*."

I swallowed thickly, the guilt I'd always wrestled with whenever I added a new one to my collection all rising up in one crushing wave. It *was* depraved. I knew it was wrong, and yet I couldn't help myself.

It had been a stupid fantasy that I'd sworn to myself that I was only going to indulge in *once,* but I was so lonely without Sebastian here, and it had gotten out of control.

"I know it's wrong. I'll stop, I swear—"

"I've already sent a photo to the Council. And to Sebastian," Deb interjected. "I know you have no parents, and I *tried* to take you under my wing and show you how to be a good partner for my son, but enough is enough. Some people just can't be helped, and you're one of them, Verity. You are just... broken. That's who you are."

She shook her head in disgust, and I mutely moved out of the way as she stalked past, pulling open the door. "Stay away from my son. Let him move on with his life; let him be *happy* for the first time in years, without the guilt of feeling like he *has* to love you just because you're an orphan who won't leave him alone. He deserves a true partner. An equal. Someone *normal*."

And with that parting shot, she was gone, leaving me alone with the collection of brightly colored tentacle dildos strewn across my bed, and a broken heart.

CHAPTER 1

G*et on your knees."*

Fuck yes, Dream Monster Daddy.

I dropped heavily to the ground, appreciating the lack of jarred knees in my smutty tentacle dream world.

"Open."

Before I could even open my mouth the whole way, a thick, smooth tentacle was sliding over my tongue, pushing my throat past what I could comfortably accommodate, making my pussy clench with need. More appendages pulled my arms behind my back, wrapped around my thighs, thoroughly pinning me in place while carefully not touching me where I needed to be touched. We'd get there, of course. This was my dream. I was just building the suspense for myself.

And yet, lucid dreamer as I was, I still couldn't visualize a face for the monster man currently reaching for my esophagus. That part of the dream was always hazy and ephemeral.

"Don't be lazy," my lover scolded, his limbs tightening around my thighs and arms in a chastising squeeze that made my cunt ache. "You can take more."

I relaxed my throat instantly, wanting to take it all, wanting to please him. My thighs tried to close of their own accord, desperate for some much-needed friction, but the inky black shackles around my legs kept them pried apart, the tip of one tentacle tickling my inner thigh, moving oh-so slowly up to where I needed it—

"Reowwwwwwwwww."

Fester's claws pricked my back through my sleep shirt as he marched up and down my spine, meowing insistently and demanding food and attention in that order.

"You're such a little demon, did you know that?" I rasped, voice hoarse from sleeping with my mouth gaping open like a fish. "I was about to dreamgasm. You're lucky I love you."

Fester peered over my shoulder to yowl indignantly in my face, blinking his enormous yellow eyes at me, which I was choosing to interpret as *"I love you too, momma,"* and also *"get up you lazy cretin."*

I knocked Fester off me for a moment as I rolled onto my back, before redeeming myself by scratching him behind the ears as I stared up at the grim gray stone ceiling above me, wishing I could go back to my psychedelic dreamland. For the most part, I enjoyed the shadow realm far more than the human realm, but I did miss color. And obviously, I hadn't found a Dream Monster Daddy in real life who'd put up with my loud voice or general weirdness.

It gave my horny dreams a bitter aftertaste when I woke up each morning. In the human realm, monster wet dreams had been purely escapist fantasy. Here, they were unfulfilled accomplishments.

Fester flexed his claws, prodding me in the boob to make me aware that I was still failing in my duties as his servant.

"Can't you catch a shadow rodent or something? I know they're here. This building is *all* cracked walls and dense overgrown vegetation. Frankly, protecting me from shadow rats seems like the least you can do. I clean your shit, you know."

Fester jumped lightly off the bed, sashaying across the room to his empty dish and stared at me, unmoved by my theatrics as I yawned and groaned my way toward him, tipping some dry cat food onto the plate.

"Don't look at me like that," I chided at his baleful expression. "I'll get you some meat from the kitchens later."

I felt bad confining him to my room—Fester had been a half-feral alley cat when I'd found him—but Elverston House wasn't exactly escape-proof, and until I was confident that every Shade in and around the palace complex wasn't going to kill the foreign animal on sight, it was these four walls for him. While he did *look* like a creature of the shadow realm with his inky black fur and glowing yellow eyes, I hadn't seen anything that resembled a cat, or even a domesticated pet, in all my palace wanderings.

It was only the proximity to the palace and clear boundary line around Elverston House that made it an appealing prospect for us ex-Hunters to stay here until we found our forever homes. It was nice to have a Shade-free space, away from the prying eyes of the court, but the building itself was one step above a ruin.

While Fester was distracted with his food, I slipped out to use the basement wash chamber—the only one that got the hot thermal water from the underground spring—and headed back upstairs to get ready, feeling somewhat more human.

"Good morning!" Tallulah sang, meeting me in the hallway and falling into step next to me. "I brought you tea! You missed breakfast in the dining hall again."

"Breakfast in the dining hall missed *me*," I corrected, pulling my door open and making grabby hands at the teacup. "Why do they serve it so early, anyway? It's not like anyone around here has a job."

Tallulah laughed, following me into my room and making a beeline for Fester—the real reason she'd come to visit. "Some of them have jobs. I guess realm management has flexible hours."

"I wish I had a job," I sighed wistfully, sipping my tea and taking it over to my makeshift dressing table.

The other ex-Hunters had jobs. Tallulah was sewing curtains and upholstering furniture to make Elverston House more comfortable, Meera was growing food and helping with pregnancy-related things for Selene, Astrid brought back supplies and was working with Austin to set up some kind of communication system for dissenters, which he did in his time off from performing. Ophelia did queen stuff—I was vague on the details, but her skills lay in her compassion and ability to talk to just about anyone.

I didn't have any marketable skills. I'd been going extra hard on generating power for the stores because that was really the only thing I had to offer the shadow realm: a seemingly limitless libido.

It wasn't exactly a hardship on my part, since the sex was great. It had taken me a while to work up to full penetration, and I still didn't let them knot me—I was saving myself for marriage—but Shade dudes were eager to please and they were all so *strong*, which worked out great for me, since I loved being tossed around the bed. Plus, they had long, kind of rough tongues and zero hang-ups about oral sex, so that was an added bonus.

If only they had tentacles. Well, they sort of did—the captain had demonstrated some shadow limbs to show me it could be done—but absolutely all of my partners had looked at me like I was not quite right in the head when I'd suggested it. One of them had told me it was beyond dated and unfashionable, which was the dumbest thing I'd ever heard.

Tentacles were timeless. Tentacles were not constrained by fashion trends, only by the smallness of the human—or Shade—mind.

That was a deep thought. I contemplated sharing it with Tallulah, but I didn't think she'd find it as profound as I did.

I was kind of horny again, just from reminiscing. Maybe I'd pick up someone at dinner, generate a little power for the realm. That could be my good deed of the day.

Wait, *was* that my job? Had I inadvertently gotten into sex work? I wasn't opposed to it, but it did feel like the kind of decision one should make intentionally.

"You could learn to sew," Tallulah reminded me. I wrinkled my nose in the mirror, parting my hair with the intention of twisting the front section into space buns, and she laughed. We'd already tried that. I didn't have the patience for sewing. And I didn't want to sacrifice my nails, so gardening was a no. I definitely didn't want to learn how to deliver babies, that was straight up nightmare fuel. Astrid point-blank refused to teach me any combat skills after I'd tried to flip a knife in my hand like they do in the movies *one time*.

"Maybe there are shadow dogs I could walk. I was a great dog walker, you know. Animals like me."

Tallulah gave me a slightly hesitant smile, clearly trying to gauge how serious I was on the shadow dogs front. Her and Meera were great—lovely, in fact—but we'd have never been friends in the outside world, and we all knew it. The only thing we had in common was whatever genetic quirk allowed us to see monsters. Meera was quiet and self-contained, and Tallulah was a motivated, creative go-getter, if not kind of a goody-two-shoes.

And I was just Verity. A hodgepodge of vague interests that I wasn't disciplined enough to turn into hobbies; vain enough to care about my aesthetic, but not creative enough to do anything cool with it; and funny, but in a self-deprecating way that had a fifty-fifty chance of making people either laugh or get super uncomfortable.

Then again, even if we *did* have things in common, I doubted I'd have been able to cultivate proper friendships with them. I had enough self-awareness to know that I was carrying around a boatload of abandonment issues from childhood, which made me cagey on the friend front. I was also self-aware enough to know I wasn't going to do anything about it.

"Maybe I could help out in the kitchen," I suggested, trying to sound more like a normal person and less like myself. "I like to cook."

"That's a good idea," Tallulah agreed hurriedly. They'd never outright said it, but I was pretty sure they both secretly thought I wasn't pulling my weight around here.

That was because they didn't know how much dick I was getting. My contributions were just as valuable as sewing curtains, right?

"I'll go ask the chef today."

"Well, maybe today wouldn't be the best." I caught Tallulah's frown behind me in the mirror. "There's a festival tonight, remember? The palace is sort of in chaos getting ready for it. Apparently, Shades from all over the realm come to see the shadow performers."

"Well, why didn't you say?" I perked up that, undoing the space buns I'd started so I could do something more elaborate. Fresh Shades were exactly the kind of excitement I needed.

Maybe if I was lucky, I'd find Fester a dad.

And if I was luckier, I'd find me a Daddy.

The festival was outside, so instead of heading straight along the path that led from Elverston House to the palace in the evening, we veered right to the extensive gardens in front of the circular building instead. As always, we were followed discreetly from a distance, and I waggled my eyebrows at a blushing Meera, who absolutely knew who our guard was. He'd been circling her ever since we'd arrived, but in a reverent, respectful way that I would have found super off-putting because I was stuffed to the gills with daddy issues and unrealistic expectations.

Meera was into it, though. She was more of a slow burner. Good for her, I guess.

"Your outfit is a hit," Tallulah said, flashing me a grin. I'd been worried the pink tulle baby doll dress, white fishnets, and bedazzled sneakers were going to be "too much," but I also fundamentally disagreed with "too much" as a concept, so I'd promptly disregarded the concern. "You look great."

"A colorful dress is such an easy win in the shadow realm, it feels like cheating, but thanks," I replied, bobbing a curtsy midstride. "And so do you—both of you."

Tallulah was in one of her own creations—she was an amazing seamstress and favored a lot of velvets and jewel tones. Usually, they were perfectly tailored, but maybe she'd made a mistake with the sizing because she kept fidgeting with the tight bust of today's dress. Meera was more of a jeans girl, but in a cool, relaxed way that I could never pull off. I was either naked, or my outfit was dialed all the way up to eleven and there was no in-between.

Unfortunately, my attention-getting outfit was having the effect of actually getting attention, which was always a bit of a double-edged sword. I was better suited to small gatherings than large crowds, and court was just one large crowd *all the time*. It was like living in a fishbowl.

If only I *felt* the confidence that I strutted around pretending to have.

"Are you okay?" Meera asked, nudging me with her shoulder. "You're quiet tonight."

"Am I? I think I'm in a contemplative mood."

Tallulah looked up in alarm. "Do I need to hide the metal again?"

"No, no. Astrid brought back that book about electricity and crushed my dreams." I still liked the idea of going full Benjamin Franklin—and trying to figure out how to turn lightning in a bottle into regular electricity so I could use my hair dryer again—but only in theory.

In practice, I was scared of storms, which was proving to be something of a setback.

"What's going on then?" Meera pressed. "What's got you feeling contemplative?"

I shrugged. "Nothing particularly out of the ordinary. Identity crisis, pondering the meaning of it all, the usual. My lack of purpose in life has bothered me since my human-realm days. It's been flaring up since you all started making names for yourself here."

"You'll find where you belong," Tallulah assured me, voice filled with conviction. "In fact, I'm confident you'll do more than that. You're too full of charisma to be destined for anything other than greatness."

She was very maternal, and while I appreciated her supportiveness, it did feel a bit like the kind of platitudes a loving mother would give her favorite delinquent child.

Tallulah knew I wasn't destined for greatness. I knew I wasn't destined for greatness. That weird-looking spiky plant over there knew I wasn't destined for greatness.

And that was fine. Some of us were solidly destined for mediocrity. It took all sorts.

"Maybe you need to take a leaf out of Austin's book and explore opportunities away from the palace?" Meera suggested, ever the most pragmatic of the three of us. "Life here at court isn't exactly full of variety."

That was true. A very particular kind of Shade lived here—the rich ones—and from our chats with Austin, they had very limited experiences with the world outside the confines of court. And Austin's life *did* sound interesting, but he had Selene to guide him. Even with my meager self-preservation instincts, navigating the shadow realm alone sounded like a bad idea.

As always, we were swarmed with suitors the moment we arrived in the garden proper. Usually, it was our little corner of the dining hall that drew all the attention, but apparently, they were going to float around us like a cloud of horny Shades tonight instead.

The fates were really not smiling down on me today because Rigel claimed the spot next to me, immediately launching into... I honestly wasn't even sure, my brain went full white noise almost instantly.

I wished I liked him. He wasn't a bad guy. He ate pussy like it was his job, kept my wine goblet full at dinner, and he'd made me a pretty shadow dress for the ball.

All signs pointed toward him being a good partner, but I had a borderline clinical aversion to things that were good for me, so a mating bite from Rigel was never going to happen.

Meera and Tallulah discreetly moved a few feet away—because they also thought Rigel was my best bet—and I turned my attention to the platters of food being circulated by the kitchen staff.

"Oh," Rigel said dully, plucking an hors d'oeuvre off a passing tray while I did the same. It was some kind of meat resting on top of a dense gray... bread? Cracker? Hockey puck? "They've started."

"Started what?" I asked absently, nibbling on the solid base and trying to decide if I liked it. I was no vegan, but it was what I imagined nut roast tasted like.

"Serving this stuff." He plucked the meat off the top and popped it in his mouth before tossing the base into a bush. "Animal feed."

I choked slightly on my gray not-nut roast. "Animal feed?"

"Supposedly, it's edible. Someone was saying that grains are a staple for Shades who cannot eat an all-meat diet for whatever reason."

Whatever reason being money, but Rigel was thoughtless in the way that people—and Shades—who'd never known so much as a sniff of poverty in their life tended to be. His snobbery wasn't malicious, just wildly out of touch.

He continued nattering about animal feed while I ate, stopping to watch a shadow artist who was creating an astoundingly realistic ocean silhouette out of shadows. Now, *here* was someone destined for greatness.

The king and queen did their formal opening speech and farewelled her guard, which Ophelia had probably told us about during our last sharing circle session but I'd forgotten about, and then we were circulating the gardens again, admiring the artwork. Rigel was hanging around like a bad smell, but I also couldn't find any more appealing prospects for my store-regeneration work tonight. I'd had high hopes for all the noncourt Shades coming to visit, but apparently, this event was more of a fun day out for the whole family deal.

How unsexy.

"Right," I sighed, bracing myself for a night of receiving great head like the true martyr I was. "Shall—"

A commotion at the front of the garden, closest to the palace doors, drew everyone's attention, silence descending over the crowd. I stood up on my toes, but I didn't have a hope of seeing above the Shades, especially with the sea of horns in the way.

"What's happening?" I asked as Tallulah and Meera sidled up next to me, a trail of admirers following behind them.

Rigel peered over the crowd before slouching down with a huff. "Nothing interesting. The king's brother is here."

Tallulah, Meera, and I exchanged confused glances. The king's brother was always here. Prince Damen sat next to the king and queen at the high table every night.

"Not that brother," Rigel clarified, seeing our confusion. "Theon. The Duke of Lindow, as he insists on calling himself," he added derisively. "Though using the lower ranking titles went out of fashion centuries ago."

A *duke*? My curiosity was piqued.

Was he single? Fester liked the finer things in life. He deserved a duke dad.

Motivated by greed, I ducked and weaved my way to the front of the crowd, dragging Tallulah and Meera along with me so I could get a better view.

Oh. Never mind then.

I'd been picturing some composite version of King Allerick and Prince Damen in my head—both of whom were strong, commanding Shades—but Duke Theon didn't look like them. Was he older? He looked old. And frail. A bit of black cloth was tied around his waist to preserve his modesty, and faint wisps of shadows floated off his skin occasionally, almost like he was leaking them. A dashing, debonair duke he was not.

He did have pretty glowing pink eyes, though. They almost matched my dress.

"You look terrible, brother," Damen said, swaggering through the crowd with a wine goblet dangling loosely from his claws. Tallulah sucked in a surprised breath next to me. Damen was usually the more personable one out of the three main dudes who ran the place—the condescending sneer in his voice was super unlike him. "Perhaps all of your arrogance and stupidity is finally catching up with you."

Holy shit, Damen did *not* like this guy. The king and Captain Soren were standing behind Damen with two guards posted at Ophelia's side, keeping her well back from the action. What was going on? Who was this guy?

"You're running this realm into the ground, *brother*," Theon spat, ignoring Damen completely in favor of glaring at the king. I guessed they were sons of the previous king, which made them all at least half brothers. "We will *starve* because of your incompetence."

"Are you too good to feed from the stores like everyone else?" Damen drawled. He waited for an answer for a long moment, but Theon wasn't giving him anything. "Ah, you *are*. You're going to let yourself starve out of pride," Damen snorted.

"Don't antagonize him, Damen," Allerick warned, nudging his heir out of the way to square off with the frail-looking duke. "Theon, don't be an idiot. If you don't feed, you'll die."

"I'm not an infant," Theon snarled. "I am not infirm. I should be feeding in the human realm like the full-grown Shade I am! You are making a mockery of everything we hold dear."

There were *just* enough murmurs from the crowd that I got the slightest bit worried. If this guy started a revolution right now, I didn't feel super great about my odds. We ex-Hunters were pretty outnumbered.

"Don't be foolish, Theon," Allerick sighed. "We have a vision for the future our world. We are creating a realm that is better and safer for all of us in the long run. Don't let your short-term greed detract from this. Everyone is making sacrifices here."

"*You're* not. You have your own power source at your disposal, ready and willing whenever you feel the slightest bit inclined to feed."

Allerick seemed to double in size, shadows flicking out in anger. "That is my *wife* and your *queen*. I have been indulgent of your impertinence already, Theon. Do not test me further."

Allerick *did* have an on-call source of fuel, and only two other Shades in the realm could boast of that privilege. And for what had clearly been a once-proud Shade, it must sting to have to go and feed from the stores again like a child...

Oh no. I was going to feel sorry for the bad guy. I could feel it in my poor-decision-making bones.

"I want a power source of my own," Theon demanded, surveying the crowd imperiously. He had a lot of presence for a guy who looked like he was going to keel over at any moment.

I liked that.

If there was one takeaway from my disastrous relationship with Sebastian, it was that I wanted a man—and/or monster—who knew his own mind.

"They aren't objects for you to claim," the king snarled, angrier than I'd ever seen him. "The ex-Hunters who reside in this realm are under the protection of the Crown, and their decisions are their own—"

"I'll do it." I stepped forward, the seam of my dress straining under Tallulah's grip as she attempted to yank me back. "I'll be on power source duty."

Ophelia was gesturing frantically behind Allerick's back, and I chose to interpret the manic slicing hand signs as approval for this very good plan of mine.

The duke seemed like a safe bet. Sure, he'd probably buff up a little after he'd fed, but overall, Theon seemed pretty harmless as far as Shades went. Plus, he was a duke, which meant he probably had a nice house. I wasn't super particular, but Elverston House wasn't the most comfortable spot.

All in all, I could probably manage him. Provided Theon didn't turn out to be a sociopathic axe murderer, this had all the makings of a sweet little setup for me, and it got me off the never-ending stage that was life at the palace.

This was probably what Meera had meant when she suggested I look for a sense of purpose outside the palace walls. Fucking this guy back into the land of the living was going to be my purpose, and I took that responsibility seriously. My dude was going to come so hard, he'll see shadows for a week.

"Hi. I'm Verity. Verity de Jager."

Theon stared at me blankly instead of falling at my feet in gratitude like he should. I wasn't some great beauty or anything, but it wasn't like he was swimming in options.

"Look, buddy, it's me or no one," I told Theon flatly, spreading my arms wide so he could get a good look at me. "No one else is volunteering."

"I think we're all trying to work out why *you* are volunteering," Damen said dryly. God, he was such a sassy-pants tonight.

That broke Theon's trance. With surprising agility for what looked to be a nearly deceased man, he darted forward, grabbing my arm and pulling me back against his chest, slowly backing away from the crowd.

"Ooh, are we playing hostage and kidnapper? I can roll with that."

"I *am* kidnapping you," he snapped. A little late to the party, but oh well. "This power source is mine now."

I rolled my eyes at Tallulah and Meera, who were staring at me open-mouthed. *This fucking guy, am I right?* I literally just volunteered as tribute in front of the whole court and a not-insignificant portion of the realm.

"I'm going voluntarily, don't worry," I reassured the royals, who all looked *very* worried. "I can't leave without my cat, though."

Or basically, anything else I owned. If I didn't have my full ten-step skincare routine, I'd turn into an angry, dry-skinned she-devil by morning. We all had our foibles.

"Verity," Ophelia said with a slightly pleading look. "Maybe we could discuss this first?"

"Oh, if you want. I'm so excited. I love a good adventure!" *Silence.* Man, tough crowd. "You guys want to come and help me pack?" I asked, turning to face Tallulah and Meera.

"Yup," Tallulah squeaked. "Let's... get you ready for this adventure."

Finally, someone was speaking my language.

CHAPTER 2

W hat do you mean I have to wait out here?" Theon demanded, glaring at Damen who was blocking the path that led up to Elverston House. "Elverston House is an ex-Hunter sanctuary, no Shades allowed."

"I'll be right out, snookums," I assured Theon, patting him on his bony arm before heading toward my dank, grim "sanctuary," a trail of ex-Hunters following behind me.

"Don't test me," Damen warned Theon as we walked away. "Look at you—you're on the cusp of death as it is."

Was that how siblings usually talked to each other? As a lifelong only child, I couldn't decide if it was cause for alarm or not.

"You don't have to do this," Ophelia said, grabbing my hand the moment we were inside the entrance hall while Astrid shut the door behind us.

"In fact, it's a fucking moronic idea and you *shouldn't* do this," Astrid added, the bitchy peanut butter to Ophelia's sugary sweet jelly.

"It does seem like it could be fun, though," Austin volunteered, grinning at me. He'd jogged after us on the way here, beaming from ear to ear. "It's a big, wide realm out there. Lots to explore."

"Stop encouraging her," Tallulah muttered to her cousin.

Meera stepped forward, picking up my other hand and giving it a gentle squeeze, staring into my eyes like she could peer into my deranged soul. "Are you sure about this, V? You don't have to go. And if you do go, you don't have to stay. Right, Ophelia? She can change her mind whenever she wants."

"Absolutely," Ophelia agreed fervently. "You can change it right now, in fact. You never have to see him again—I'll deal with it. Theon doesn't come to court, you won't run into him."

"You all worry too much," I replied breezily, wriggling out of their grip and practically skipping up the stairs. Well, skipping on the inside. On the outside, the years I'd dedicated to avoiding cardio meant stair skipping was an impossible feat. "Did you see him? Theon *needs* me."

Astrid groaned from her position at the back of the small, unsupportive crowd that was apparently accompanying me to my bedroom.

"Verity," Tallulah began patiently. "It's not your job—"

"Right, right, he has to want to fix himself. Totally. I get that. He seems very *passionate* though, right? I do like that in a man."

"Perhaps we should just focus on the 'leave whenever you want' idea," Austin suggested mildly, cutting off whoever was about to lecture me next.

Fester met us at the door, meowing indignantly, either because I had the audacity to leave or because I had the audacity to return.

"Hello, baby," I cooed, scooping him up and nuzzling his soft little head. "Are you excited to meet your new dad? He's a bit grumpy, but you'll win him over. Maybe we'll make you a big brother one day."

I wasn't totally unhinged. I was pretty sure that I was just going to go have some mediocre sex with a listless Shade until he perked up, maybe hang around for a couple of weeks while he enjoyed having me on tap, then he'd get sick of me and send me on my way. I didn't *actually* think we were going to get married and have adorable hybrid babies. Mostly, I just wanted to see how far I could push it before Astrid burst a blood vessel.

"Here, say your goodbyes," I instructed Tallulah, depositing Fester in her arms before pulling my suitcases out from under the bed. I'd definitely brought more possessions from the human realm than my roommates, and I'd probably requested more from Astrid's supply runs than anyone else as well.

I just liked *stuff*. If maximalism was wrong, I didn't want to be right.

"Maybe you should just take the essentials?" Tallulah suggested. "Treat it as a trial run for a couple of days."

"Everything is essential," I told her solemnly.

"In that case, there are some boxes downstairs you can use," Meera said, already heading out with Austin in tow.

While everyone was radiating disapproval, they didn't hesitate to jump in and help. Meera and Austin taped together flattened boxes, and Tallulah, Astrid, and Ophelia helped me dismantle my room, packing everything up far more neatly than I would have, while periodically taking breaks to snuggle Fester.

He acted like he was aloof, but he was secretly loving all the attention.

I dumped armfuls of clothes into a suitcase, ignoring Tallulah's wince at my lack of folding, before climbing up onto the dresser to untack the sheer pale pink fabric I'd draped around the walls.

"I hope Theon likes pink," Astrid said dryly, picking up the puddle of material as it slithered to the floor and folding it into an unnaturally perfect square while looking at it like it was going to bite her.

"His eyes are pink, did you notice?" I asked excitedly. "It feels meant to be."

"Nope," Astrid announced. "I refuse to let you entertain the idea this is fated because I want you to feel one-hundred-percent confident in leaving if you change your mind. Do not hang all your hopes and dreams on this dude, okay? It could be a disaster and if it is, there's no shame in leaving."

Aw. We may not have anything in common, but I really loved this little crew of misfits I'd found myself in. As far as kind-of friends went, I could have definitely done worse.

I jumped down, standing in front of Astrid and giving her my most sincere smile. "Can I hug you?"

"Yes," she grumbled, though her posture relaxed slightly. "But only because it's a special occasion."

Someone sniffled as Astrid pulled me into her embrace, squeezing me tightly despite her complaining.

"Will you come visit me?" I asked her, wrapping my arms around her waist. Holy muscles, Batman. I should work out sometime. Astrid was *built*.

"Try and keep me away," Astrid replied. "And if *Duke* Theon doesn't treat you well, I'll kick his ass. Deal?"

"Deal."

By the time we emerged with rolling suitcases and stacks of boxes and a quiet, watchful Fester contained in his carrier, another Shade had joined Damen and Theon outside Elverston House. He appeared to be quite old with deep wrinkles and silvery strands in his hair, though in better shape than Theon was.

"Wilder, at your service, miss," he said, hurriedly stepping forward and attempting to take the carrier from me. "The Duke's attendant."

"I've got this," I said, holding Fester a little closer to me. "Nice to meet you, Wilder. I'm Verity. This is Fester," I added, holding the carrier up a little so they could see through the mesh.

Fester eyed them balefully, silent and watchful. He only got chatty when he was more comfortable. Theon was eyeing him right back, equally as wary. Clearly, it wasn't love at first sight for either of them.

"I'll arrange some extra help in transporting your stuff," Astrid volunteered. Soren was hovering not far away, observing the situation from a distance, and Astrid made a beeline for her mate.

"Come," Theon announced. "Say your goodbyes."

"Your see-you-laters," Ophelia corrected, giving him a withering look. Queen shit, right there. "As we fully intend to see Verity regularly."

"Yes," Damen agreed. "In fact, I think I'll swing by tomorrow, Verity. See how you're settling in."

"You're not invited," Theon said rudely.

"Too bad," Damen shot back cheerfully.

"I'm sure it won't be a problem for Damen to stop in and check on me," I cut in. For a Shade on the verge of death who was relying on this arrangement going ahead, Theon was a real uncooperative little asshole. "Will it, *Your Grace*?"

Theon gave me a flat stare, glowing pink eyes giving nothing away. "If he must."

"There we go, all sorted. Let's be on our way then." I beamed at him, and he gave me a look that was perplexed at best.

"*Are you sure about this?*" Astrid mouthed, narrowing her eyes at Theon as we passed her, heading for the nearest entry room.

I shot her a thumbs-up, which only made her scowl even harder. Truly, there was no pleasing some people.

I'd never seen Theon at court or even heard his name mentioned, but he certainly seemed familiar with the layout of the grounds, seamlessly leading us to the entry room while bypassing the main gardens where the festival was still raging on. Well, the process of avoiding everyone was seamless, whereas the journey itself was actually pretty labored, since Theon didn't appear to be doing so well.

I almost opened my mouth to suggest we take a break, but he must have anticipated my question and shot me a look so indignant that I decided to just let it go. If he wanted to suffer, that was on him.

"So, shall we get to know each other?" I asked cheerfully. "My name is Verity de Jager, I'm thirty-two. Been in the shadow realm awhile now, yet to find gainful employment. I'm open to job suggestions if you have any."

Theon shot me a sidelong look, heading into the entry room first without bothering to hold the door open behind him. Not the most chivalrous of dukes, that was for sure.

"Your job will be to feed me."

"Just to clarify, you know that means sex, right?" I asked bluntly. He *looked* like a hermit, and I wasn't sure if he'd gotten the memo that the Hunters' source of power resided somewhere in their reproductive organs, unlike regular humans, who gave up the energy goods through fear.

"I'm aware," he clipped.

He didn't seem too enthused about the idea. Damn it, boring Rigel and his dedication to oral were looking better by the second.

"Are you going to tell me about yourself?" I asked, shifting the weight of the cat carrier from one arm to the other and wondering if I'd been overfeeding Fester.

"I am Theon, Duke of Lindow."

I waited, but no other information was forthcoming. Way to give me nothing, dude.

The door closed behind me, immediately ensconcing us in darkness. "You're going to need to hold my hand or something. I can't navigate the in-between the way you can," I told him. I could feel my way to a portal, but the random entryways dotted all around the place were only accessible by some kind of internal compass Shades had.

"Hold... your hand?" He made it sound like I'd just asked him to pop a particularly gnarly pimple for me. It didn't bode well for our sex life, that was for sure.

"Just shepherd me somehow," I sighed. Theon must have been standing closer than I realized, and I startled as his clawed hand wrapped cautiously around my wrist, tugging me along with him.

If it sucks, you can just tell Damen tomorrow that you changed your mind, I told myself, steeling my resolve. *And if it doesn't suck, well at least you've got some purpose now.*

I was about to be the most satisfying lay of this dude's life.

CHAPTER 3

My intention when I'd stormed Allerick's party tonight had been to secure an exemption for passage to the human realm so I could feed at will, his idiotic rules be damned. As the former heir, and technically still third in line to the throne, I shouldn't be subject to all of these ludicrous restrictions. Besides, Allerick would be thrilled if I was killed in the human realm, never to darken his doorstep again.

But this... this colorful, loud, interesting power source I'd brought home with me...

This was much better.

I didn't need to go back to the human realm to feed. *My* power source—my *Verity*—would be living under my roof and I was never going to let her go.

And one day, when I finally overthrew Allerick and took the throne for myself, she would be *my* Hunter queen. Yes, that was a wise course of action. The realm needed continuity, and a Shade king with a Hunter queen provided that.

It had been very wise of me to kidnap her for myself. Besides, she was... pleasant to look at. Pink. Bright. And she had such interesting, decorated claws. My sister would find them fascinating.

My sister would have to wait, though, because I was *very* hungry.

Did Hunters require privacy to service Shades? I supposed that wasn't too much to ask. I could at least show her to her room before I requested her attentions.

"Come," I commanded, *feeling* the phantom shadows ushering her forward, though I was too hungry to actually form them. What a sorry state of affairs Allerick had let the realm fall into. I would have never allowed such things to be had *I* inherited our father's crown.

I would have found a way to bring all of the Hunters here by now, and after enough time in the shadow realm, they would learn to enjoy being the Hunted again. We would be fed, they would be content—the ones who'd come here already seemed perfectly happy—and the natural order would be restored. It was baffling that Allerick hadn't even attempted such measures.

At the very least, I would have bribed more of them here by now. My brother was such a lazy ruler. His strategy seemed to be: let whoever wanted to come show up when they felt like, and, in the meantime, let the realm starve.

Begrudgingly, I could admit that I had no idea about the history of the connection between Hunters and Shades until my informant at the palace had relayed it to me. While it was merely good fortune that Allerick had stumbled upon this far superior source of power, he'd at least had the good sense not to squander his queen when he'd discovered what she could do.

The problem was that his current method of dealing with the Hunters—a lunatic organization whom he should have never attempted a treaty with in the first place—was going to be the death of us all.

No one wanted to talk about it, but I would. The stores were dwindling. When they were empty, Shades would die en masse.

"It's raining," Verity said unnecessarily as we stepped out of the entry room, hidden away in the trees near my home.

"It rarely isn't."

This was a particularly lush, verdant region, in large part because of how much it rained.

"Whoa," Verity breathed, looking up at my home as we broke through the tree line. "This is nearly as big as the palace."

I bristled. "This is the original palace, and it is far older and of greater historical importance than the hideous, oversized one the *king* lives in."

Verity looked up at me with wide, unblinking brown eyes, carefully shifting the bag containing her small pet beast from one hand to the other. "I'm sensing some sibling tension here."

"Why would I feel any kind of tension? I am superior to my brother in every way." *Except for raw strength, apparently.* "My sister will give you a tour of the castle later. For now, I will show you to your room."

"Okey dokey."

"You do realize that you are my captive now?" I confirmed, because Verity didn't seem to understand the magnitude of her situation.

"Right, right. I volunteered to be your captive." The corner of her mouth twitched, and the motion was quite enchanting.

"You clearly didn't know what you were volunteering for. You are my captive. You will live here forever, and I will feed from you at my leisure."

"Well, if you say so." She shrugged dismissively.

Perhaps the Hunters weren't very intelligent?

All the more reason for us to have rounded them up long ago. For their own safety, if this one was anything to go by.

Wilder would bring her things through the servants' entrance, but I took my time showing Verity through the front door. Partly to let her appreciate the ornate architecture and grand entryway, and partly because I was finding it difficult to walk at all. This route allowed me to take more natural stops for Verity to admire her new home.

Aderith appeared from the servants' entrance next to the stairs, inclining her head respectfully and watching Verity with unabashed curiosity. She and Wilder had all but raised me since birth, not much shocked them anymore.

"Aderith, this is Verity. I have stolen her from the palace. She is to feed me and will be my queen when I take over the realm."

"Very good, Your Grace."

"Excuse me?" Verity spluttered, staring at me with interestingly wide eyes. "Can we cool it on the treason?"

"Absolutely not. Verity, Aderith is my seneschal. She will show you to your room. Second floor. The east-facing one," I added quietly.

Aderith blinked, the only sign of her surprise. There was only one east-facing room on the second floor, and it had never been used during my time. Before they could leave, my sister appeared at the top of the stairs, surveying Verity coldly.

"What is *that* doing here?" she asked disdainfully.

"Wow," Verity laughed, a loud, bright sound that echoed off the walls. "Way to make a girl feel welcome."

I was slightly taken aback by her confidence. Melody-Rainywillow wasn't quite of age yet, still a child to our kind, but she could gut Verity with almost no effort.

That idea made me... displeased.

Rainy stayed here by choice, unshakeable in her belief that she would overthrow me someday and be the mistress of this house—a notion I had encouraged because I wanted her to be strong and self-assured—but she was still technically a guest at this point. Perhaps I should send for Mother to collect her for a few weeks, just until Verity was settled in.

"This is Verity. You will treat her with respect."

"No, I won't." Rainy flounced off in a blur of shadows, slamming her bedroom door behind her.

Aderith's gaze tracked her, disapproving. She had always warned me that I was too indulgent when it came to Rainy. "Come, Verity. I will take you upstairs."

"Um, sure," Verity replied faintly.

My gaze lingered on Verity's back as she climbed the steps, admiring the shapely curves of her body, though I couldn't help but wonder how such a fragile being would be able to take me. Would it be enjoyable for either us? I imagined not. Sex was not an act I had much bothered with thus far. The types of lovers that a former, now disgraced, crown prince attracted were usually not the kind that I took any pleasure in spending time with.

I was allowed to plot against my brother, but I wouldn't allow the crown to be disrespected by anyone else.

Once Verity and Aderith had disappeared to the second story, I began the ascent myself, pausing every few moments to steady my shaking limbs. We could not go on like this. The energy stores were low as it was, and they weren't for fit, healthy Shades like me. They were for children and the elderly. For invalids, who would struggle to feed any other way. It was an insult to the strength and independence of every full-grown Shade to even suggest they drain community resources in such a way, and I'd thus far managed to get by without sacrificing my morals.

But barely.

The shadow realm deserved far better than Allerick's irresponsible idealism. We needed *strength*. We needed a leader who was willing to make difficult decisions and face the wrath of unhappy citizens when it was the right thing to do.

The shadow realm needed *me*.

CHAPTER 4

That was the duke's sister," Aderith murmured, leading me in the opposite direction the young Shade had gone. "Melody-Rainywillow. She lives here."

It took me a minute to place it, but eventually I remembered where I'd heard her unusual name before. This was the teenager Austin had told us about once in an ex-Hunter wine-and-cheese gossip session.

Her attitude had sounded a lot funnier when I wasn't on the receiving end of it.

"I guess I'll get to meet her properly later then. How long have you worked here?" I asked Aderith, hoping I sounded cool and casual as I tried to get the lay of the land.

Historically, I wasn't great at reading people—or Shades—so that I was struggling to figure Aderith out wasn't all that surprising. I was definitely curious about both her and Wilder though. Were they cool with all of Theon's... Theon-ness? Were they anti-Allerick too? I guess it wasn't out of the realm of possibility since Captain Soren's sister had accumulated a whole ragtag army of rebels at one point.

Aderith glanced back at me over her shoulder. "Wilder and I have been married for many decades. The former king asked us to run this household for his infant son and presumed heir."

She turned away, a clear sign that she didn't want to discuss it any further. Was... was *Theon* the infant son? He'd once been the heir? I guess the anti-Allerick stuff made some sense in that context. It was like sibling rivalry on steroids.

Aderith led me to a nondescript wooden door at the end of the landing, pushing it open and gesturing for me to enter. Fester had been very quiet in the carrier, though I felt it shifting in my hands as he stood and moved around.

It was a nicer room than I'd had in Elverston House. Smaller, but that was okay. The stone was paler and less grim looking, and the curved ceiling made the place feel more intimate. The bed was an enormous four-poster monstrosity with heavy gray velvet drapes—not exactly my aesthetic, but I could roll with it—and there were nooks and wide window ledges all around the walls that Fester would have a ball with.

"There is a bathing chamber through there," Aderith said, gesturing at one of the three wooden, coffin-shaped doors. "Shall I run you a bath?"

"Just show me how it works, I can run it myself." I deposited the cat carrier on the ground, confirming the door to the hallway was closed before letting Fester out to take a sniff around.

"This is Fester. He's very friendly, I promise," I told Aderith, who looked less than impressed as I quickly set up his litter box. "I mean, he can basically be bought with meat, so he's pretty easy to manage."

Fester immediately sprang up onto the window ledge, narrowly avoiding an ornamental candle holder, and yowling loudly in disapproval.

"I know, I know. Wait here, Momma is going to figure out how to use the bath."

"That's a strange-looking ostecta," Aderith said, hovering by the bathroom door.

"A what? Fester is a cat. From the human realm," I clarified when she only looked more confused.

"Ah, I see. On reflection, I think I may have encountered these animals on my trips to the human realm to feed."

"What's a... ostecta?" No one had ever mentioned them to me before, but then again, no Shades had actually *seen* Fester since Shades weren't allowed in Elverston House, let alone my bedroom.

"A similar creature, but with eight eyes—spread all around its head— and longer, sharper teeth that protrude below its jaw."

Well, that sounded horrific. Like some sort of cat-spider-sabertooth nightmare.

"They do not live inside homes," Aderith added disapprovingly. "They are wild beasts who make their homes in the forest."

"Fester was a wild beast once," I replied sincerely. "A wild, feral alley cat on the mean streets of Denver."

Aderith looked impressed. "And you tamed him?"

"Sure." If by *tamed*, she meant *bribed with food until he loved me.* I didn't want to ruin the impression that I was a total badass, though. It was a smidge dishonest, but it might come in handy for them to think I was tougher than I was.

Maybe some of Astrid's frustrated warnings had penetrated the *all vibes, no stress* fog that usually permeated my brain.

"Do you think he'll be able to roam around inside?" I asked Aderith. "He's very friendly, and he was so bored being cooped up at court."

"There are no other animals within these walls to harm him," Aderith responded cautiously. "And the doors and windows are always shut against the rain. However, I would advise you give His Grace time to warn his sister first..."

Noted. No letting Fester out until the sister was under control.

The faucet above the bath required some manual pumping, but steaming hot water came out which was a nice perk—no basement trip required. Aderith excused herself to put fresh sheets on the bed while I holed up in the bathroom, Fester sitting on the wide ledge of the circular tub to supervise and scold me for disrupting his schedule.

"I know, I know." I stripped out of my tulle and fishnets, peeling slightly damp panties down my legs because my savior complex had manifested in my vagina. "But he *needs* me. And it's nice to get away from court for a little while, don't you think?"

Hopefully, the wooden door was thick, or Aderith had a front-row seat to my one-sided conversation with my cat. Then again, she seemed to be the nonjudgmental type. Surely, they'd have to be to live with Theon and Melody-Rainywillow, neither of whom struck me as the cool, no-drama sorts.

"Remember when you were just a sad little street cat, hissing and scratching everyone and everything?" I asked Fester, lowering myself into the steaming tub. "And I showered you with love and food and turned you into the charming young man you are today? That might be my superpower. I fixed you. *I can fix him.*"

I tipped my head back against the ledge, careful to keep my hair dry. Somewhere in the depths of my psyche was a warning voice telling me that I was on the fast track to misery again, but I was great at ignoring that. When I wanted to put on rose-tinted glasses and turn those red flags into parade decorations, I really committed.

But this was different. Theon wasn't Sebastian.

Sebastian would have never claimed to have kidnapped me—or fake kidnapped me, or whatever was going on here. He would have jokingly told everyone that *I'd* kidnapped *him*, or that he'd been trying to shake me off for years but couldn't get rid of me. I'd always introduced him as my "better half," and he'd all "tee-hee, I just found her wandering around outside and she won't leave me alone," and all his elitist college buddies would laugh and laugh, and I'd smile so hard it felt like my face was going crack in two while I died of embarrassment on the inside.

In the hour or so that I'd known Theon, I had already established that he was riddled with flaws, but I didn't think that would be one of them. And it wasn't like I didn't have flaws of my own. Theon would see them soon enough, and probably ship me back to Elverston House to molder away the remainder of my hottest years in a crumbling ruin.

Aderith was gone by the time I climbed out of the cooling water. I dried off, wrapping myself in a towel, and headed into the maze of bags and boxes my room had become. Wilder had clearly been busy. Huh. How was I going to get *stuff* now? I'd become reliant on casually mentioning things I needed—in the very loosest sense of the word—to Astrid whenever I ran into her around the palace, and then they'd just magically show up outside my door sometime later.

Maybe I could have a standing shopping order for hair and beauty supplies, scented candles, Fester's food, and bath bombs. I was a simple girl—so long as I could feed my cat, slather my face in absurdly expensive retinol, and drown out the smell of my sorrows with frangipani and sea salt candles, I could be happy anywhere.

After hunting through my things, I managed to find my pepto-pink fuzzy bathrobe and matching slippers, fully intending to get properly dressed into something sexy after I'd warmed up a bit.

I doubted Theon was going to need any encouragement—his options were basically fuck me or die—but I still wanted to make an effort.

Saving lives was good, honest work, and I wanted to treat it with the respect it deserved.

I shoved a few boxes around to make a walkway between the three doors and the bed, eager to pull out the swathes of pink fabric and hang them on the walls tomorrow. This room desperately needed a pop of color once I had some space to move around in.

Closet, I decided, making for the third door. I'd fill the closet with my everyday pieces and then figure out how to organize the rest.

Except when I opened the wooden door, I didn't find the storage space I'd expected to find.

I found a staircase. A narrow, winding stone one that led upward, faintly illuminated by a silver orb somewhere above me, though I couldn't see where.

Carefully pulling the door shut behind me so Fester couldn't escape, I started the climb, keeping my hand flat against the rough-hewn wall for balance. Was this some kind of servants' passage? That could be handy, especially if it led to the kitchens. Though presumably, those would be *down*stairs, not up.

It didn't take me long to find myself in front of another wooden door. Surprisingly, it opened easily, swinging out to reveal a *far* fancier bedroom than the one I was sleeping in directly below.

"Ah," said Theon from the middle of the biggest bed I'd ever seen. "Good, you've come to service me."

I blinked at him before looking down at my fuzzy robe, and slippers and then at the staircase behind me. "There's a staircase directly between our rooms?"

"Of course. You are in the... *inamorata* suite."

I burst out laughing before I could stop myself. "Oh my god, I'm in the mistress dungeon for easy access? That's kind of genius, honestly. Will you be sneaking down to me in the middle of the night, or should I expect summons upstairs?"

"It's not a *dungeon*," Theon spluttered indignantly. Seeing him off-balance really changed his whole face, made him look much younger and more approachable.

Plus, he had *such* pretty pink eyes. And his horns were *so* curly.

What did he look like when he was well-fed and at full power?

"I thought I was your prisoner. Surely, you'd want me in a dungeon."

"I *have* a dungeon. *That* is not a dungeon."

"Right, right. I don't want to disrespect the courtesan holding cell. Mistress storage closet? Whatever. Let's do this then. Any preferences? Hard limits? I'm pretty open-minded, but no knotting. I'm saving that for my mate."

Mostly because I hadn't encountered anyone I wanted to be physically attached to for longer than five minutes.

Theon harrumphed. "No. You have permission to do whatever is required to adequately feed me."

"Hot," I muttered sarcastically, kicking off my slippers and shrugging down my robe.

Theon's gaze tracked my every movement as I climbed up at the bottom of the bed, crawling up next to his legs. It was more for my benefit than his. I liked putting on a show, and I kind of needed to turn myself on, because Theon wasn't giving me a whole lot to work with. I mean, yeah, it was hot that he was looking at me, but a little dirty talk wouldn't have gone amiss. Even better would have been some firm instructions. Or just throwing me down on the bed and having his way with me, but Theon was clearly in no condition for that.

I did appreciate the way his gaze roved over my body, though. That was nice.

"I'm going to touch myself," I informed him, presenting myself with a little more confidence than I felt. I *loved* sex, but I absolutely did not love taking the lead. Every moment had me second-guessing, wondering if they were even into me, if I was doing something wrong, if I looked stupid, or if my face was doing something weird.

I loved when my partner took all of that noise away. When they demanded and I submitted, and there was nothing but pleasure.

But, alas, this wasn't about me. Not this time, at least.

I straddled Theon's leg, not actually touching him, and slid my hand down my body. Despite the thick layer of awkwardness coating this whole interaction, I wasn't surprised to find my pussy already damp as I slipped my middle finger inside, dragging my wetness up to my clit.

That was my superpower: my vagina's Pavlovian response to even the possibility of sex.

"I can already feel it," Theon rasped. "The power coming from you. Just a taste of it in the air..."

"Maybe you'd feel it more if I was touching you?" I suggested, never entirely sure when the feeding mechanism kicked in.

"Yes, I think so. Sit your cunt on my thigh."

Say what now?

Maybe I wouldn't need to take the lead quite as much as I thought. I lowered myself down, spreading my arousal over his leg while I continued to tease circles around my clit. In all honesty, my fingers weren't doing a ton for me—I'd probably ruined myself with toys over the years because my digits felt weak and insubstantial in comparison—but a warm, solid *thigh*? Now that I could grind on.

"Move your hand out of the way. Pleasure yourself on me," Theon demanded.

Oh, *now* we were cooking with fire.

I didn't want to brace myself on his body because he looked like I could crush him, so I leaned over slightly to put my palms on the mattress and started rolling my hips, angling my pelvis forward so my clit had some much-needed friction.

Theon inhaled deeply, a low grumbling sound emanating from his chest. "Your scent... Is that fear?"

"Nope. That's *all* arousal, my friend."

Theon gave me a strange look. "For me?"

I'm surprised as you are, buddy. My gaze caught on the thick outline beneath the small piece of fabric he'd knotted around his waist, and my mouth watered slightly.

He didn't look frail there.

"May I?" I asked, tugging gently at the bottom of the material.

He shredded it with his claws, exposing a cock the length of my forearm lying semierect against his stomach, and slick *gushed* out of me, sliding over his leg onto the mattress.

Way to play it cool, pussy.

"You are pleased," Theon observed smugly.

"There's plenty to be pleased about," I murmured, grinding myself down a little harder and wondering if I could actually fit that inside my body. I didn't shy away from a challenge—I had some *huge* dildos, but they were stationary objects, and I could control exactly how much I took.

There were a few more variables when the giant dick was attached to a real-life being.

"Bring your cunt here. I will ready you with my tongue."

"Like... *on* your face?" I verified.

"Yes, Verity. On my face."

Usually, I took a very *if he dies, he dies* approach to face sitting, but Theon looked like he might *actually* die, which gave me pause. But only a little. I crawled up the bed next to him, swinging my leg over his face but keeping all of my weight on my knees, and braced my hands on the headboard. Theon's horns dug into my waist, forcing me to drape myself over them slightly, adding an extra layer of eroticism. There was no forgetting that the male underneath me was no human when his horns were propping me up.

With his long tongue, it didn't matter that I was holding myself up slightly, but apparently, Theon wasn't satisfied with that. He grabbed my ass from behind, claws digging into my cheeks as he yanked me downward, his rough tongue instantly filling me.

I let out a muffled shriek, burying my mouth in my forearm at the last minute. He didn't seem quite so fragile now. His hands held me in place as he licked everywhere he could reach, from clit to ass, then back to tongue fuck my pussy some more. With each passing moment, he seemed to grow a little more energetic, his hands holding me a little tighter.

How fast was I feeding him? Did it work that quickly?

"On my cock," Theon snarled, dragging my ass backward too fast for me to steady myself. I landed on my back between his thighs, legs draped over his body, entirely splayed out for him.

I startled at the difference already. The hollows in Theon's cheeks and under his eyes had filled out, making him look far younger than he had just a few minutes ago. His shoulders were bulkier too, and the bones of his chest were no longer visible.

Had *I* done that?

Goddamn, I was powerful.

Now it was *him* crawling over *me*, a menacing look in his glowing pink eyes that probably shouldn't have had me clenching around nothing.

He wrapped his clawed hand around the gentle curve of his yet-to-inflate knot, giving it a squeeze while staring between my thighs like I was housing the most magical thing he'd ever seen.

"You are going to be an addictive little treat, my captive."

He rubbed the thick head of his cock around my clit for a moment before sliding it down and pushing it in, inch by glorious inch. Slick was running down my ass, pooling on the bed beneath me, easing his way, but *fuck*, it was still incredibly intense.

He was so *big*, I could feel him everywhere.

"I can't—"

"Yes, you fucking can," Theon growled in my ear, leaning down and nipping at my lobe. "You can take it. Grab your legs, pull them up for me."

I obeyed instantly, my eyes rolling back as the movement pushed him a little deeper.

"Mm, look at you," Theon murmured, gaze firmly trained between my thighs. He rocked his hips forward, and I let out a muffled moan at the sight of him sinking into me. My hand came to rest on my lower abdomen, just out of curiosity, to see if I could feel him there.

It was like pouring gasoline on a flame.

Theon thrust forward with one rough movement, and I *absolutely* felt his cock under my palm and just about everywhere else. To my surprise, I was clenching around him instantly, an orgasm that I hadn't seen coming, ripping through my body like a tornado, my mouth open on a silent scream.

For all his initial excitement, Theon slowed down, keeping his thrusts gentle and shallow for a moment while I rode out the waves of pleasure. My mouth was dry, dehydrated from the gallons of slick I was producing. With each gentle roll of his hips, my thighs shook, toes curled into the sheets, every nerve in my body responding to his movements.

Theon groaned, a deep, rumbling sound of pleasure that set me off again. He took over holding my legs, picking up his pace. He was thicker and stronger everywhere, with shadows rising off his skin like steam. A totally different Shade to the one who'd interrupted the festival a couple of hours ago.

My head spun like I'd been drinking, a warm, heavy, lethargic feeling spreading through my limbs.

"You have four horns now," I slurred, staring dreamily up at him.

Theon paused, staring down at me before muttering to himself, "I'm taking too much."

With impressive ease, he gathered me in his arms and guided us back, draping me over his body with him lying on his back, his cock still buried somewhere around my spleen, no knot binding us together.

"Shh, rest." His voice was oddly soothing, a clawed hand stroking the back of my neck. He reached for a glass bottle on the nightstand, easily popping off the lid with one hand and holding it to my mouth to drink. The water was cold and soothing, and more of it spilled down his chest than went down my throat, but it immediately helped.

"Close your eyes, my captive. Rest a moment."

Gosh, that was sweet. Had I gotten him all wrong? I hadn't been expecting a soothing, gentle, romantic Shade to be hiding underneath that prickly exterior.

"Because you won't be any use to me if you're dead," he added affectionately, patting me on the butt as I drifted into sleep.

CHAPTER 5

I hadn't even come yet, and I already felt better than I'd felt in *years*. Healthier. More alive.

This little Hunter was the key to everything. I refused to believe that Allerick could possibly be stronger than me when I had her energy coursing through my veins.

Then again, I'd made the mistake of assuming Allerick couldn't possibly be stronger than me before, and lost my position as heir because of it. I wasn't going to make the mistake of overconfidence again.

Verity made an odd snuffling noise in her sleep against my chest, her mouth slightly parted and body covering me like a blanket. Unfortunately, I'd perhaps been a little too greedy with her in my need to prevent my imminent death. My cock had softened slightly inside her, but not entirely. The moment she had enough strength to continue, I would see that she had my cum.

It felt imperative to me, somehow, that she receive it. Perhaps I would spill on her skin, since she didn't want me to knot her. Rub it into her flesh so she walked around smelling like me.

Yes, I was fond of that idea. That in itself was slightly alarming. It wasn't something that had ever held any appeal to me before. This small, loud creature had affected me more than should have been possible.

It was just the sudden power coursing through my veins making me feel overly sentimental.

After an hour or so of me musing about what this new development meant for my plans, Verity roused, blinking up at me in confusion.

"More water," I ordered, holding out the bottle for her.

She took it and sat up, drinking without question. How pleasantly obedient she was.

I took the bottle once it was empty, setting it back on the nightstand.

"I'm not done with you, little captive." I maneuvered Verity onto her back, my cock already rising to the occasion. "I didn't finish. But I'm not going to feed anymore."

"You can turn it off?"

"I believe so." I'd stopped when I realized she was starting to get woozy. It was *instinctive* to stop, my body hadn't allowed me to take more. "Are you sore?"

"Nope." Verity's thighs fell open, revealing that pretty cunt I wanted to taste again. She was very enthusiastic. Had I gotten particularly lucky in my choice of Hunter?

The scent of her desire was far more potent than the smell of human fear had ever been. *Of course*, this was what Shades should be feeding on. It seemed only natural that we did.

I shuffled back on the bed, licking her clit roughly until her slick was flowing again, needing just one more feel of her pussy gripping my cock before I would finish on her breasts.

She came with a cry on my tongue, and as much as I wanted to drink down every last drop of her slick, I needed to keep her pussy nice and soaked for me.

"Let's see if you can take it without whining this time."

Verity's eyes flashed with defiance. "I can take it."

She bit down hard on her lip as I fed her each hard inch of my cock, breasts rising and falling temptingly with each breath. She took me beautifully, in truth, her delicate body seemingly made for mine, soft smooth stomach bulging as my cock slid home.

How was I meant to get any of my work done when I had this temptation living under my roof?

Verity smirked, far too cocky for someone as thoroughly impaled as she was. She didn't even have real claws! And her teeth were blunter than a newborn Shade's. It was unfathomable that she possessed any confidence whatsoever.

Some of that cockiness faded as I picked up my pace, replaced by a needy, drunken expression that I found myself quite fond of. Yes. I would like to see her look like this each morning and evening, and I would never so much as feel a hint of hunger again. I would never need to experience the indignity of taking from the stores, stealing from the Shades who actually needed those resources to live.

As Verity lost herself to her pleasure, she tilted her head back, exposing the smooth column of her neck to me.

And my teeth *ached*.

I ran my tongue over them, wondering if they'd always felt that long and sharp. Every instinct in my body screamed at me to bite her, to sink my teeth into her throat, and I had no idea why. It wasn't an urge I'd ever experienced before.

And I wasn't in the habit of denying myself the things I wanted.

I lowered my head, opened my mouth, and captured the junction of her shoulder and neck between my teeth, biting down until coppery blood filled my mouth.

"Theon!" Verity shrieked, her pussy clenching and pulsating around me. "Fuck, fuck, fuck."

My knot was swelling, and I vaguely recalled her not wanting that, so I started pulling out, hating the feel of leaving her perfect, slick cunt.

"What are you doing?" Verity snapped, grabbing my ass with her delicate, breakable fingers and attempting to yank me back to her. "You may as well knot me *now*."

I was confused by her tone but not about to question it when she was offering me what had suddenly become the thing I wanted more than anything else in the world. With one rough thrust, I enthusiastically shoved my knot forward as I came, greedily watching Verity's every reaction as it swelled to its full girth inside her.

"Oh *fuck*," she slurred, pretty brown eyes growing unfocused. "It's so big."

It had been twenty years since I'd had a lover, and I'd never knotted anyone, but I suspected that my knot was thicker than most. My chest puffed out with pride at the acknowledgment.

Verity shifted experimentally, milking more cum from my cock and setting off another wave of clenching, whining orgasms for her. Fuck, the *sounds* she made. Desperate, greedy, *whimpering* sounds.

If anyone else heard them, I'd have to kill them.

"Do you know what you've done?" Verity asked, struggling to catch her breath. Her breasts heaved with the movement, and I dipped my head, intending to drag a taut nipple between my teeth.

"Focus!" she scolded, grabbing my chin with frankly astounding boldness, and yanking my head up. "Do you know what you've done? Do you know what that bite means?"

I dropped my gaze to it, admiring the still-bleeding wound on her neck. Perhaps I should lick that instead. Yes, that was a good idea.

"Oh my god, hornball, you are so easily distracted. That is a mating mark. You have *mated* me. Do you know what *that* means?"

"It doesn't matter what it means. You are my captive, and I am keeping you forever, regardless."

"Yeah, no shit you're keeping me forever. We're fucking bonded by some kind of... I don't know. Magic or something. Whatever. We're basically married. We're more than married. We're *super* married."

She sounded worried. I ground my pelvis against her clit, letting my knot soothe her back into a state of mindless calm.

"You... can't... distract... me... with...*fuck*!"

I laughed darkly, delighted with my new little *mate*. I hadn't intended on getting married, but why not? A wife who fucked like a dream *and* kept me at full strength while doing it? No Shade would turn down such a gift.

Though I couldn't deny that there was a faint thread of concern working its way through my elation. What did having a mate entail? What limitations did it impose? How long would it take for the bite to heal?

"Okay, but now we really have to talk about this," Verity gasped, cunt still fluttering around me. "What are we going to do?"

Interestingly, her hesitation erased mine. "You are going to live here as my mate, and I will see to your material needs while you provide power when I require it. What more is there to discuss? I can hardly *un*bite you."

Verity narrowed her eyes at me, face flushed red and covered in a fine sheen of sweat. I found I liked her this way. If I could, she would look this well sated always.

"So, you're just...*fine* with this then?"

"What's not to be fine with? As far as I can tell, this is in every way to my advantage," I pointed out. Verity huffed indignantly. "What is it you require to be content here? A grander room? A separate wing for your pet beast, perhaps? Some special foods? Jewelry? Name your price."

Verity's expressions were odd to me, but I hazarded that she looked considering.

"I am one of the wealthiest Shades in this realm. I will take care of you in all ways. And you will feed me and stay here with me. Make your demands, my captive."

"Honestly, when you put it like that, it doesn't sound *so* bad... Can I be bought? Yes. Maybe." I didn't respond, since she appeared to be asking the questions to herself. "And this knotting thing. How often do I get this?"

"As often as you like."

Verity nodded solemnly, and I wondered if I had stumbled upon the most delightful being in the entire realm.

"I want Fester to be able to roam the house safely. Everyone has to know not to hurt him."

"As you wish."

"And I like the mistress storage dungeon, but I want to decorate it however I like."

"It's not a *dungeon*—" I began, exasperated.

"And I want to be able to visit the palace whenever I please."

"Absolutely not," I growled. "You are my *captive*."

"No, I'm not. I will be visiting my friends, Theon," she warned in a delightfully aggressive voice. "We can pretend I'm your prisoner all you like, but you are not trapping me here."

That didn't sound satisfactory at all. The palace was where that smug prick Damen always was, and he wanted my Hunter, I could tell. The whole court was crawling with Allerick's sycophants, and they would *all* want my Hunter. No, no, that would not do.

"How about I will escort you to the palace when you wish to go?"

"What if I want to go every day?"

"I have a throne to take, Verity." This disjointed, barely functioning realm wasn't going to run itself, and it was clear Allerick wasn't going to do it—not well, at least. "I will escort you there, twice per week at most."

She nodded smugly, and perhaps I had not negotiated that well. Her reaction implied she was expecting much less.

Usually, I was an extremely strong negotiator. Verity was very distracting.

"Well, cool. I guess we're life partners now—"

My knot softened, and the sudden gush of liquid distracted her from whatever she was going to say. I reached between us, cupping her pussy, suddenly very irate that any of it was leaving her body.

Verity swallowed loudly, staring at my hand between her thighs as I pressed my cum back inside her with my palm, careful not to break her delicate skin with my claws.

"Squeeze your thighs together," I ordered, taking my hand away, entirely unsure where these new possessive urges had come from. Presumably, a side effect of the mating mark that needed further investigation.

But if I was going to change the shadow realm for the better, then I needed to get back to work. I didn't have time to spend pondering these new developments.

I climbed off the bed, taking one last moment to admire her. Verity's hair was a mess, her skin covered in a thin sheen of sweat, cum leaking profusely from between her slick-coated thighs. She was a sticky, messy disaster, and it was intensely attractive.

What a novel feeling.

"Now what?" Verity asked, though the question seemed loaded somehow. I couldn't help but feel like she thought I was doing something wrong, though I couldn't possibly deduce what that might be. I didn't make missteps.

"Now you entertain yourself while I return to my work," I told her, because wasn't that obvious? With a curt nod, I exited the room, heading down to my workshop with Verity's slick still coating my skin beneath my shadows.

A very successful evening indeed.

63

CHAPTER 6

Theon shut his bedroom door behind him, leaving me sitting in the sodden mess that was his sheets, an ache between my thighs and a still-bleeding throb on my neck.

Mated.

I was *mated*.

On the *first fucking night*. Theon really did not waste any time in securing the permanency of his mistress storage dungeon occupant.

Mated.

And here I'd been, naively thinking that I could *manage* Theon. Clearly, that had been a mistake. I doubted there was a being in this realm or any other who could manage him.

Tentatively, I walked my fingers up my neck, surprised to find the raised bump of scar tissue already forming, the blood that had seeped from the wound mostly dry.

"What the fuck," I whispered, my heart rate picking up slightly. The speedy healing and lack of pain were pretty disorienting on their own, but combined with the overall weirdness of the whole situation, and I was totally adrift.

And yet... not filled with regret either. I mean, that would probably come in time—perhaps when I was better acquainted with the stranger I was now bonded to for life—but at the moment, I was feeling weirdly smug about the whole thing. I could recognize that there were some toxic impulses at play—it was nice to feel wanted, to drive him so out of control that he'd sunk his teeth into me, to finally feel like I *belonged*—but whatever. Maybe the toxic hole of abandonment issues was just where my brain lived now and I could be fine with that.

Wincing at the knot-related ache between my legs, I climbed off the bed, ducking into Theon's far-larger, grander bathroom to do a cursory cleanup so I didn't leave a trail of slick down the secret stairs, before wrapping myself back in my robe and tucking my feet into my slippers. He clearly hadn't expected me to stay here, so I headed back down to my room, a little of the smugness wearing off with each careful step on the narrow staircase. I didn't need us to stay up late braiding each other's hair and talking about our feelings or anything, but a *little* aftercare would have been nice and made me feel less like a fleshlight with bonus charging capabilities.

I let myself into my room, startling at the sound of running water. Aderith poked her head around the bathroom door, gesturing for me to come in.

"I thought you might want another bath."

"That sounds amazing, thank you." My face was on fire at the thought of poor Aderith being subject to whatever sounds I'd been making up there. The whole knot situation had definitely busted my brain-to-mouth filter.

Aderith nodded before doing a double take, her gaze trained on my neck, a look of abject horror on her face.

"What has he *done* to you?"

Oh. She was worried for *my* sake?

"It's a mating bite," I replied hurriedly. "It's okay. It doesn't really hurt. It's already healing."

"But *why*? Why did he do that to you?"

On reflection, Theon hadn't seemed fully informed about the whole 'mate' concept either. Since he never spent any time at court and seemed to despise everything about his brother, maybe all his information about the ex-Hunters was secondhand gossip rather than cold, hard facts.

"The mate bond is a connection between Shades and my kind," I explained, fumbling slightly over the words. "It's like... a supernatural thing, I guess. Tethering us together for life. Like marriage, but more permanent."

Now that I was focusing on the strange new sensation forming in my chest, I realized I could probably follow it directly to Theon if I wanted to. It felt like a magnet, drawing us together.

Aderith looked stricken, which was frankly a far more reasonable reaction to have than Theon's had been.

"But you just met!" She walked past me to pace alongside the bed. "This is very bad, Ver— *Your Grace.*"

I blinked. "You really don't have to call me that. Verity is fine."

"It will be 'Your Grace' in front of *His* Grace," Aderith muttered, still pacing. "The king will not be pleased at this turn of events. He is very distrusting of his brother, you know."

"I can't imagine why," I replied mildly, heading into the bathroom because there was a real situation happening on my inner thighs. I left the door open so I could still hear Aderith, and stripped off my robe, climbing gingerly into the steaming-hot tub.

"What will you tell the court?" Aderith asked, raising her voice slightly so I could hear her from the bedroom. "Wilder says that Prince Damen is coming tomorrow to check on your well-being."

"Shit," I mumbled, tipping my head back against the lip of the tub and closing my eyes. I'd forgotten about that.

She was right, of course. The king *would* be pissed about this sudden development—he was adamant that the ex-Hunters who came here take their time in choosing a mate, if we chose one at all, and that we never felt pressured into a relationship by anyone.

Theon had taken a *slightly* different approach.

"Perhaps it would be best if we didn't raise this with Damen tomorrow," I hedged, immediately feeling guilty for lying. "I'll just wear a high-necked top and we just... don't have to talk about it. It's not like he's going to ask, right? I mean, it's barely a lie."

"I think that would be for the best," Aderith replied, sounding equally as discomfited. "Why don't I go fetch you some tea and food? You must be... hungry. After all that."

Famished. It didn't *hurt* when a Shade fed from me, but it did take a lot out of me.

"That would be amazing, thank you."

Maybe Theon sucked at aftercare, but Aderith was absolutely crushing it. I could live with that.

"Good morning, handsome," I cooed, scratching behind Fester's ears as he yowled in my face. "First day as a mated lady. Shall I go introduce you properly to your new dad later? He's very grumpy, and I think he's probably going to be imprisoned for treason one day, but maybe we'll still get to live in the nice, fancy house."

I clambered out of the absurdly high bed, wincing at the lingering ache in my nether regions. Knotting was really a whole different ball game. Muscles that had never been stretched in their life were getting a serious workout.

I fed Fester before letting myself into the bathroom to get ready for the day, though I had no idea what I'd be doing, but by the time I finished my hair and makeup, I was ready for another lie down. Dressed in pale pink loungewear with a high neck that covered my bite, I climbed back onto the bed, flopping down on the pillows. Theon must have been *really* starving last night because I was absolutely tapped out.

I didn't want to be all moon-eyed about it, but what was he doing right now? Was he thinking about me? I had to have crossed his mind at least once, surely. Then again, he'd been more than happy to vanish the moment his knot went down, and it apparently hadn't bothered him that I'd slept in my own room.

Though, why would it? Theon wanted me for what I could do for him, not for *me*. Best to keep that idea firmly at the forefront of my mind at all times. At thirty-two, I was now pretty convinced that my prefrontal cortex hadn't developed and never would, and I'd be doomed to make poorly planned decisions for the rest of my existence, but even *I* knew it would be a bad idea to catch feelings for the Duke of Lindow.

Fortunately, his piss-poor attitude made that a lot easier.

"Verity," Aderith called tentatively, tapping gently on the door. "Prince Damen is here to see you."

I groaned as I rolled out of bed, tugging the neck of my sweater higher. I quickly undid the high bun I'd pulled my hair into, letting my curls bounce free for added neck shielding.

Aderith led me downstairs, shooting me a warning look over her shoulder as I fussed with my neckline again, and I took the hint and pinned my arms at my side. Fortunately, Theon had opted to bite me right where my neck met my shoulder, which was one of the easier spots to hide, as far as throats went.

Shit, I probably should have mentioned to Theon that we shouldn't say anything. I didn't think he'd take it too well if Damen demanded I leave, and he was treasonous enough as it was.

Perhaps I didn't have anything to worry about. Damen appeared relaxed as I came down the stairs, lounging against the wall like he belonged there, while Theon brooded silently in front of him with Wilder at his back.

The difference between the Theon who'd stumbled into the party and the Shade standing in the foyer was jarring. He seemed to have tripled in size overnight. His skin was smooth and glowing, and his eyes a more vibrant pink.

This Theon didn't look like he needed to be fixed. He looked like he could crush me if the urge took him.

He was also really fucking hot. I hadn't had a chance to appreciate that particular bonus of my new mate last night. My face heated as he stared at me, tracking my every movement.

"Hi!" I said brightly to Damen, bobbing a clumsy curtsy at the bottom of the stairs. I never remembered what the etiquette was, but no one had told me off yet. "How's it going? Nice of you to stop by."

I was talking too fast. Damen, Theon, and Wilder were all staring at me. At this rate, I was going to be the one to give the game away.

"How are you, Verity?" Damen asked carefully, narrowing his eyes when Theon took a wide step sideways, angling himself in front of me. "You're looking much better, Theon."

"Indeed. This arrangement suits me very well."

I preened a little at the noncompliment.

"I don't care about you," Damen replied, back to his nonchalant self. "Verity, could I speak to you privately?"

"Absolutely not," Theon growled. Oh man, my inner toxic queen was totally fist pumping at *that* show of possessiveness.

Damen sighed. "You're going to be difficult about this, aren't you? If you can't show self-control, Verity can't stay. We need to be certain that she's safe."

"So ask her," Theon grumbled, gesturing at me.

"Because I'm sure she'll feel completely comfortable answering honestly while you're standing there glowering," Damen replied cheerfully. "Verity, are you happy to step outside with me for a moment?"

"Of course."

I wished I'd put shoes on. I felt extra small and out of my depth in my pink sweats, matching high-necked sweater, and polka-dot socks.

Theon grabbed me around the waist as I passed him, hauling me back against his body.

"Don't forget who you belong to," he growled, his voice so low I could barely make out the words.

It was like he'd hacked into my brain and found the master key that unlocked all of my deepest, darkest desires.

Theon inhaled deeply and I closed my eyes in embarrassment, realizing my scent had given away just how much I liked those words.

I attempted to hold my head high as he released me and I followed Damen out of the front door, but I wasn't sure I was pulling cool, calm, and collected off. My brain was a cocktail of emotions, and I hoped I wasn't about to say something stupider than usual and ruin this whole arrangement.

Damen's body language was open and friendly as he gestured for me to sit on a stone bench on one side of the long porch, a thick gray hedge growing up behind it keeping the rain at bay. His posture was in stark contrast to the way Theon presented himself, and if I hadn't heard them refer to each other as brothers, I'd struggle to believe it. They carried themselves like they were from different worlds.

Damen sat on the other end of the bench, both of us angled toward each other. I had no idea what to expect of this conversation since my interactions with the crown prince had been pretty limited. He'd attempted to get to know all of us when we arrived—presumably in the search for a mate of his own—but our chats had been stilted and filled with awkward pauses. Tallulah said she'd gotten nervous and started oversharing, while Meera had sat in almost total silence when it had been her turn. If Damen was looking for love, he'd been pretty unlucky so far.

"Verity," Damen began, calm as can be. We weren't friends, but from that one word, he made it sound like we were. "Talk to me. How's it going? It was a pretty spontaneous decision you made to come here. If I may be blunt, your scent seems to indicate you're comfortable in Theon's presence."

Shit, shit, shit. This felt like a job interview, and I'd never been good at those. If my scent was doing something weird, Damen politely didn't comment on it. I felt like it was, though—aside from the lingering horniness, I was nervous as hell, and my mating mark itched underneath the fleece sweater like it wanted to announce its presence.

"I'm doing great." I cleared my throat, aiming for a lower octave. "I'm doing great. I'm very comfortable here. Theon has been the perfect... host."

I'd briefly entertained the word "gentleman" but I didn't think I could get that one out with a straight face.

"It's the very least he can do," Damen replied dryly. "Considering what you're doing for him. Verity, it's important that you understand that you have all the power here—literally and figuratively. You can leave whenever you want."

"Right." The mating bite went full Pinocchio's nose, growing itchier with my lie. "But I can also stay, right?"

"I won't pretend it's ideal," Damen laughed, lounging back on the bench. "But Allerick is thinking long-term. *Happy* ex-Hunters in the shadow realm is his priority. Otherwise, how can he convince more of you to move here? That's the question—are you *happy*, Verity?"

"Sure. I mean, yes." I laughed, an annoying nervous reflex I'd never managed to get rid of. "It hasn't even been a full day yet. Can I have a little more time to decide?"

"That seems like a fair request." Damen stood, his smile as pleasant and unreadable as ever. God knows what he was going to tell the others when he got back. "I'll be stopping by every couple of days just to check in, and obviously, you're more than welcome to return to the palace whenever you like. I can accompany you—"

"Theon has already promised he'll accompany me back. Twice a week," I added, pushing myself up from the bench.

"Has he now?" Damen murmured. "That's an interesting development. In any case, I'll see you in a couple of days."

"Great."

Damen gave me another long look. "You should know if you're staying here that Theon has some ideas about how the realm should be run that Allerick and I don't agree with."

I snorted at the understatement. "I gathered that."

Damen nodded. "He's not a threat—we'd have never let you come here if we were worried about your safety—but he will... well, he'll talk a lot of shit. Just remember that he's a sad, bitter old man, and don't take any of it seriously. Until next time, Verity."

Damen walked down the front steps, not bothering with going inside to say goodbye to Theon.

I lingered on the porch, frowning to myself as I watched him leave. Could I have developed Stockholm syndrome when Theon wasn't *really* my captor? Because I didn't like the way Damen had spoken about him at all, and I was feeling really compelled to run after the prince and defend my new mate's honor.

Theon yanked the door open before I could touch the handle, grabbing my upper arms and dragging me inside. He instantly nosed the fabric of my sweater out of the way, horn brushing the side of my head as his tongue snaked out to trace my mating mark.

I nearly melted into a puddle in the foyer.

"Do not speak to him again."

"That's not an option and you know it. Don't be so bossy."

Wilder discreetly slipped out of the entryway, leaving the two of us alone. For a house this large, there was a surprising lack of staff. I'd only seen Wilder and Aderith so far.

Theon walked me backward, pinning me against the wall, tongue still playing with the raised skin of the bite.

"Did you tell him about this?"

"I thought it best we... not," I replied lamely.

"Aderith mentioned as much."

"What is your problem with Damen anyway?" I asked breathily, tilting my head back to give Theon better access. The Allerick thing I got—it had to be jealousy, right? Courtly intrigues and whatnot. And Allerick wasn't exactly Mr. Friendly, but Theon could hardly judge on that front. Everyone liked Damen, though. He was the least scary Shade at court.

Was it just a power and prestige thing?

"I don't have a *problem* with him. I don't care about him at all."

"Liar," I breathed, trailing my hands up the sides of his face, desperate to touch those horns.

A knock at the door right next to me startled us both, and I banged my head on the wall at the sudden sound.

"Ow." I rubbed the back of my head while Theon pulled me away from the wall, hands on my forearms, looking at me like I was about to collapse at any moment. "I'll be fine, give me a minute."

Aderith appeared, seemingly out of thin air, looking between Theon and the door as though silently asking if she should open it. He hesitated, and it was very clearly because of my presence.

"I'll just be upstairs," I said, excusing myself with what I hoped was a convincing smile. I didn't want to get in his way. And I wasn't sure if I even wanted to know what kind of visitors Theon had. Fellow treasonous plotters, presumably. Probably best to steer clear of those.

"Verity," Theon called after me, his voice low and commanding. I paused midway up the stairs, looking back down at him. "I'm not done with you, my captive."

That feeling was entirely mutual.

CHAPTER 7

The moment Verity's door clicked shut behind her, Aderith opened the front door and I huffed out a frustrated breath to find Tanix standing on my porch again.

I dismissed Aderith with a wave of my hand, not wanting her to be subject to this nonsense.

"I thought I'd gotten rid of you."

"We're not giving up, Your Grace. We believe in you. In your vision for the realm."

If it were anyone else, I'd have been thrilled at the show of support. But Meridia's leaderless band of rebels was more hindrance than help. They craved trouble and lacked discipline.

I'd also heard about their confrontation with the captain and the queen's sister, which made me more uneasy than ever before at Tanix's presence. I didn't want him near Verity.

"We heard you confronted the king in front of everyone at the Festival of Shadows. It gave us hope we've scarcely had since Meridia..."

"Don't speak of her," I snapped. I wanted to overthrow my little brother. I wanted to see him kneel at my feet and admit that I was stronger and wiser and better suited to rule, the way I'd had to when I'd lost his challenge all those years ago, in front of the whole court and our father, who hadn't so much as looked at me since that day.

I'd been all but banished, a formerly beloved crown prince, now forgotten by everyone.

But that was the extent of the suffering I intended for Allerick. I didn't want him dead. And I didn't want to hear the name of his would-be assassin said in my presence.

"There is nothing for you here," I reiterated. "I want order. You want chaos. Our views are not in alignment."

"Your enemy is our enemy," Tanix shot back, refusing to take the hint.

"My *obstacle* is your enemy," I corrected. "Leave here. You only missed Prince Damen by minutes, and he will be back. You were foolish to come."

That made Tanix straighten. He was a fugitive, as were Meridia's other known followers. They split their time between desolate campsites and the darkness of the in-between to evade capture, which was probably why he was so persistent. An extended stay in the in-between would be enough to make any Shade lose hold of their sanity.

"Come find us when you are ready, Your Grace. We will be your loyal followers until the very end."

I slammed the door shut in his face, now even more irritated than I'd been when Damen showed up. The utter contempt Meridia's followers showed for the traditions of this realm was infuriating. Where was their honor? When I won the crown back for myself, it would be because I'd proven myself, and the realm would be on my side. I had no interest in stealing it through treachery.

I'd almost demanded a rematch with Damen when he'd shown up here this morning, the first since he'd defeated me in a challenge years ago. Did he not think I was capable of looking after my own Hunter? My own *mate*? Verity was fine. She would live comfortably here. I didn't need to be supervised like an errant child.

Unlike my sister.

I'd come down here to channel my frustration into something productive, but Rainy had beat me to it. She was skulking around in the shadows in a high temper, waiting for me to acknowledge her presence.

Was everyone determined to frustrate me today? Perhaps I should have gone up to my room and called for Verity instead. She hadn't irritated me yet.

"What is it, sister?" I grumbled, walking around the wooden workbench that dominated most of the space to make sure she hadn't touched anything. "Speak quickly, then leave me. I am not in the mood for company today."

Rainy landed with a light thud, having climbed up to one of the upper shelves for her tantrum as she did when she was a child.

The urge to summon Mother to deal with her grew stronger.

"It's not fair."

"What isn't?" I asked absently, internally listing several things in *my* life that weren't fair. Namely, that Allerick was stronger than me, followed by the fact that Damen was also stronger than me. The course of my life had been set, I'd already been raised as a future king.

And then *they'd* come along.

Verity should be living the pampered life of a queen, with an entire retinue of attendants to see to her every whim.

"My entire *life*, I've been waiting for the day when I could finally go to the human realm and feed for the first time. *Every* Shade gets to do this. It's a rite of passage. A sign of adulthood. I won't *be* of age until I've made the trip, so why can't I go?"

"Because the king is cowardly and lazy, you know this."

I wasn't unsympathetic to my sister's plight. That first trip to the human realm was something every Shade grew up dreaming of—whether they were fearful nightmares about being chased through the dark by knife-wielding Hunters, or fantasies of exploring a realm that was so very different from our own. Rainy had grown up hearing stories of the human realm, as well as receiving an extensive education on how to safely feed, where to feed, how to escape Hunters, and so on. She'd *trained* for this moment, we'd planned exactly where she would enter the human realm for the first time, and now it was being snatched away from her.

"So, why do we listen to him?" Rainy challenged, glaring at me from the other side of the workbench. "Why should we?"

"Because."

"Because *why*?"

I missed the days when she was an infant and couldn't challenge my authority. In truth, I didn't have a good answer at hand. While I felt that Allerick's course of action was directionless at best, I wasn't about to send my baby sister out to defy his mandate. I was always acutely aware that if Allerick defeated me again, he didn't have to be as gracious as he'd been last time. At least I'd gotten to keep my home before, there was no assurance I'd receive that grace again.

No, if I was going to outright move against his rule rather than merely demand he change it, I had to be *ready*. I had to prove that even if I didn't have the exact physical strength to match my brother, I had a more comprehensive vision for the future of the shadow realm. I would make up for whatever they perceived that I lacked with intellect and a bold approach to solving problems that Allerick could never match.

"Can you not simply do as I say without arguing?" I sighed. Was it too much to ask that everyone just do that?

"No. And you can't stop me. I *will* have my moment. Tradition *will* be upheld," Rainy declared, stomping out of the room and slamming the door shut behind her. I closed my eyes for a moment, exhaling heavily. I didn't like to send my sister away, but Mother had the ability to guilt Rainy into behaving. It never worked when I tried it.

"Wilder!" I called, leaning my head out of the door and waiting.

He stepped out of one of the servants' entrances a moment later. "Yes, Your Grace."

"Send for my mother to come and collect her daughter."

In hindsight, perhaps Mother moving out of my home before Rainy was of age had been a poor choice. But her own father had died two years ago, and she'd taken up residence at her family seat—which would be Rainy's someday if she failed to overthrow me for this one. Rainy hadn't wanted to move, but it would do her good to spend some time there.

Mother certainly couldn't stay here. She would be far too intrigued with Verity, and I had no desire to share my mate's attention.

"Of course," he said quickly, moving faster than I'd seen him move in years.

I suspected that both Wilder and Aderith preferred when Rainy wasn't here, though they'd never said as much. They had been assigned to me by my father when I was born, and caring for Rainy had never been part of their remit, but they'd done it anyway, even when she'd been at her most difficult.

I'd been too lenient on her all these years, allowing her ego to grow far beyond anyone's control. While I wanted to protect my sister from anything that might cause her discomfort, I suspected that only being truly humbled would improve her attitude at this point.

Satisfied that Rainy was dealt with to the best of my abilities for now, I pulled the heavy blanket off my latest experiment, exposing the system of empty glass orbs connected by thin silver wire. I'd had to give up working on it while my own power levels were so low, but my skin was vibrating with excess energy now.

I added a small amount of ignition powder to each of the orbs before screwing them tightly together so they would glow when combined with my energy. Usually, they were fed shadows manually and topped up as needed; though that was infrequent, they could glow for weeks.

I'd deliberately used less powder than I would for a regular orb, as I didn't want these for illumination purposes necessarily. I wanted them for *messaging* purposes. If I could get the timing down to a precise art, as well as ensure the connection *between* the orbs was perfect, then this would be the basis of my safety system for Shades. I would create paths throughout the in-between, and scouts could go ahead to the human realm, checking there were no Hunters in sight before lighting this beacon to alert those waiting to feed back home that the location was safe.

It would be faster and more responsive than the scouts merely relaying information by walking back and forth—a sometimes time-consuming journey. And if an area became compromised, the orbs could be extinguished to prevent others from beginning their trip.

Unlike Allerick, some of us were actually *doing* something to solve our current crisis.

Aderith appeared with a plate of meat at some point, leaving it on a side table for me while I tinkered with the orbs, trialing different amounts of ignition and recording my results. Silver was a good conductor of our powers— our strength and our weakness—so I felt moderately confident in my ability to light them all in a chain reaction. Extinguishing them was the conundrum. And if I couldn't instantly extinguish a pathway, this was all for naught. Safety would be compromised, and I would not allow that.

Frustrated that the solution hadn't just appeared in my mind yet, I turned around to grab a piece of meat, only to find myself staring into the yellow eyes of Verity's small beast, hunched over my plate. With a challenging glare, it snapped up a large piece between its dainty pointed teeth, staring at me as it backed away with my lunch in its mouth.

Why was it roaming around the manor as if it owned the place? *Stealing* my food?

"Halt, beast," I ordered, glaring at it. It paused, glaring back at me while gnawing on my food. "I am the lord of this house."

It was fast, I'd give it that, but I knew every nook and cranny of this workshop. With some cajoling, I had it backed into a corner where I instantly pounced, snatching it up into my arms, keeping its limbs trapped to its body so it couldn't catch me with its sharp little claws. What an odd creature for Verity to want to keep as a companion.

"Come along, beast," I said, stomping out of my workshop and up the stairs. I could already hear Verity's loud voice carrying from the small, informal dining room where she was undoubtedly taking her meal, uninterrupted by this thieving little creature.

"Verity," I said gruffly, closing the dining room door behind me and depositing the creature on her lap. "This was in my workshop, stealing my lunch."

"Fester!" she scolded, though she was holding him close to her body, nuzzling the top of his small head with his chin. It hardly seemed like a punishment. "How did you even get out of my room, you little sneak?"

"Did I not already agree that he was free to roam?" I grumbled, though I had no idea why I was reminding her of the fact.

"He needs a couple of days in one room to settle in first," Verity replied absently, stroking the purring creature in her lap. "Though he seems confident enough, doesn't he? Fester used to live on the streets, it took me a while to coax him in and get him to trust me. He's still got those street cat instincts."

It seemed very apt that Verity had coaxed a feral animal off the streets to be her pet. She seemed to be sorely lacking in defensive instincts, though it had worked out well for me, so I wasn't about to complain.

"I'll get you another plate," Aderith told me, straightening from where she'd been fussing over Verity's tea. "Will you take your meal in here, Your Grace?"

I usually took my meals alone in my workshop, fully absorbed in my work. Perhaps establishing a tradition of taking our midday meal together in here would be sensible. It seemed wise that I keep an eye on this new mate of mine for deteriorations in her physical and emotional condition, or any sign that she was going to try and leave.

Yes, a daily meal together would be a good idea indeed.

"Yes, I will eat here. Verity and I will take our midday meal in here together each day."

Verity raised an eyebrow as Aderith slipped out of the room. "Will we now?"

"We will."

"How nice of you to ask me," she snarked, not an ounce of deference to be found.

It didn't bother me as much as it should.

Aderith appeared and quietly set down a fresh plate of meat for me, pouring some tea before letting herself out of the room. I watched as my mate held the teacup up to her chin, the steam wafting off the top doing something pleasing to her golden-brown skin. Making her look... glowy.

"So what's all this about then?" she asked, setting Fester down. He immediately rubbed himself against her legs before roaming around the room, poking into corners and wriggling under the buffet. "Why the regular meals? Were you missing me?"

"Of course not." I couldn't quite hide my abject horror at the concept. I'd never *missed* anyone in my life.

"Sure you weren't." Verity shot me a coy grin, brimming with confidence. She never responded the way I expected her to, and it entirely threw me off-balance.

"I simply felt it would be practical for us to take a daily meal together, so I have decided that's what we shall do."

"Well, if you've *decided*, then I guess there's nothing more to be said," Verity remarked mildly, watching me over the rim of her cup before taking a sip of her drink.

"That's obviously correct," I agreed, though somehow she'd made it sound like it wasn't obviously correct and it had me second-guessing myself slightly.

Which was ludicrous, I never second-guessed myself.

I ate in silence, watching Verity do the same and making a note to ask Wilder to enquire at the palace about the food offerings for Hunters. She seemed content enough with meat, but perhaps there were other things her fragile body required?

As though I'd summoned him with my thoughts, Wilder slipped through a servants' door, giving us a curt bow.

"Any response from my mother?"

"She has already sent for your sister. I delivered Melody-Rainywillow to her immediately. I'm here because you have received an invitation from the palace to dine with them tomorrow evening, Your Graces."

I sighed heavily. Had I not suffered enough?

Verity looked at me, frowning slightly. "Do we need an invitation? Anyone can eat in the hall, right?"

"Only those who live at court," I corrected. "But I'm assuming this particular invitation is for a private dinner."

"That is correct, Your Grace," Wilder replied. "A private invitation from the king."

"This is your fault," I muttered to Verity. "Usually, the king goes out of his way to avoid my presence."

"You're welcome," she replied sweetly, as if my words had been meant as a compliment. "Ooh, what am I going to wear?"

Wilder looked at me, waiting for confirmation either way to give to the palace messenger who was undoubtedly waiting in the foyer.

I had no particular desire to go, spending time at the new palace only ever served as a reminder of everything I'd lost. But Verity looked... excited. Presumably, it was some unwelcome side effect of the mating bond, but I disliked the idea of taking that excitement away from her.

"Fine," I agreed. "Tell them we'll attend."

"Very good, Your Grace," Wilder murmured, inclining his head respectfully as he backed out of the room. Verity was far more jovial for the remainder of lunch, while I sunk into an increasingly worse mood. Was the idea of spending time with them really so appealing for her? Why was *my* company not enough to make her smile and chatter like that?

Why did it even bother me that it wasn't?

CHAPTER 8

I don't think your new father likes me," I whispered conspiratorially to Fester as I finished getting ready for dinner at the palace, pulling my hair back on one side into twists, encouraging my curls to sit firmly on the left side of my head to help with bite coverage.

Fester opened one eye, staring down at me from the high ledge he'd sprung onto, before closing it again.

"He didn't pull me out of storage at all last night," I continued. "And the only time I saw him all day was for lunch, and I got three grunts and an order to eat more meat. What do you think that means? Because *I* think it means I've already irritated him, and he's having second thoughts but he's also supernaturally stuck with me now."

I added a few silver braid cuffs to my hair twists and double-checked that my scar wasn't visible beneath my baby pink jumpsuit. It was sleeveless, with a high neck and bow, and I'd paired it with shiny silver pumps that were just the right amount of tacky for my tastes. They also matched the new press-on nails I'd spent the afternoon applying, which were a soft pale pink, and covered in diamante swirls.

"Oh well, at least I'll have some company at dinner. Not that you aren't wonderful," I assured a dozing Fester. "It's just that your conversational skills could use a little work, you know?"

He deigned to give me an offended look as I left the room, my heels clacking loudly on the stone floors, disturbing his sleep. I triple-checked the door was shut behind me before heading down the stairs, following the sound of raised voices to the foyer.

"You're not coming," Theon insisted, glaring at an enraged-looking Rainy, and an older Shade that *had* to be their mother—she had the same pink eyes and curling horns, though hers were daintier than Theon's.

"There she is!" she squealed. "Come here, come here. Let me look at you."

Hesitantly, I headed the rest of the way down the stairs, ignoring Rainy's death glare and smiling tentatively at the Shade in front of me who was all but bouncing on her feet with excitement.

"Ooh, look at your claws!" she cooed, grabbing my hand to admire my bedazzled nails. "How pretty!"

"Careful of your own claws," Theon snapped. "Her skin is delicate."

"Of course," she replied, immediately contrite as she peered soulfully at me. "Did I hurt you?"

"No, not at all." Honestly, I hadn't picked Theon for such a worrywart. "I'm Verity, by the way."

"What a beautiful name. Theon and *Verity*, how lovely," she sighed dreamily. My face burned so hot, I was surprised steam wasn't rising off it. "I'm Xanthia, Theon and Rainy's mother. It's *such* a pleasure to meet you."

"And you," I replied dazedly. She was so *nice*. So bubbly and enthusiastic and the complete opposite of both of her children.

"I confess, we're being a little naughty," Xanthia said, leaning in and speaking in a low voice. "We overheard the invitation to dinner at the palace yesterday, and Rainy and I are trying to convince Theon to bring us along. I haven't been to the palace in years—in solidarity, you know—and I would *so* love to go."

"Mother," Theon sighed, looking every bit the put-upon son. "It's not my dinner to invite you to."

"Oh, they won't mind," Xanthia said, gesturing absently. "The king is hardly short of food or space. Simply send Wilder ahead and ask them to set two more places. Wilder, darling, would you be so kind?"

Wilder grimaced, looking to Theon for his instructions. To my shock—and I suspect everyone else's—Theon looked at me. Presumably, because I had the most recent experience at the palace and knew the king's temperament better, but still.

It was a little weird.

"I'm sure it wouldn't be a problem," I hedged.

Xanthia squealed, jumping up and down. "Then it's settled! Rainy, my sweet, you do promise to behave, don't you?"

Rainy, who'd been staring at me like she could disperse me into shadows with her eyeballs, nodded once and unconvincingly.

"Wonderful. Oh, this will be so fun!"

Theon muttered his instructions to Wilder, and I couldn't help but think that the look he was giving his mother was oddly guilty. Maybe he felt bad that she hadn't been to the palace in a while when she was clearly so thrilled by the idea.

It was reassuring to know he was capable of feeling guilt. That he wasn't just all crazed tyrant beneath his grumpy surface.

Wilder bounded off ahead as the four of us made for the entry room. To my surprise, Theon was at my side the moment we stepped out the door, offering me his arm as I balanced precariously in my pumps on the uneven ground. As though it was second nature to him, he formed a thick layer of shadows above our group's heads like an umbrella, keeping the steadily falling drizzle off us.

"Thanks," I murmured, resting my hand lightly on his forearm, marveling at just how strong and solid he felt beneath my palm. The physical changes he'd undergone in the past couple of days still astounded me.

Theon grunted, grabbing my hand and settling it more firmly on his arm, giving my impractical shoes a judgmental look in the process. "You smell... pleasant."

I raised an eyebrow at him, trying to decide if the words had been a compliment or an observation.

"Why is it you really want to attend this dinner?" Theon asked, turning his attention to Rainy.

"I wish to tell the *king* myself how unfair I find his travel restrictions," Rainy huffed. "And ask him for an exemption for all young Shades needing to travel to the human realm for their first proper feed, as tradition dictates."

"Oh, Rainy," Xanthia sighed, giving her daughter an indulgent smile. "I do so admire your independent spirit, but could you not wait for a more opportune time to bring up such a topic? It really will put such a dampener on the dinner conversation."

"I don't care about *dinner conversation*, Mother," Rainy shot back indignantly.

"Well, you should. You're a daughter of the nobility, you'll either inherit my family seat or overthrow your brother for his one day. Social graces are important, my darling."

Rainy muttered something too low for me to catch, though judging by the warning look Theon gave her, he caught it.

"Aren't you worried if you go hunting in the human realm that you'll... you know, die?" I asked.

Rainy snorted, giving me an unimpressed look. "The more time I spend around Hunters, the more I'm convinced we have absolutely nothing to fear from them."

I laughed. The absolute brass balls on this kid. "Easy to say when you're flesh and bone and teeth and claws."

Rainy opened her mouth to argue but Theon cut her off. "Sister, you have never been to the human realm. You cannot comprehend how truly vulnerable we are in that form until you have experienced it. In their realm, we are *helpless*."

"I wouldn't be," Rainy argued stubbornly. "I'm fast. No Hunter would be able to catch me."

The two of them continued to bicker as we entered the in-between, Theon keeping a firm grip on me the entire way while I silently regretted my choice of footwear.

"Theon has always been like this with all of his siblings," Xanthia told me with a happy laugh. "It's how he shows his affection."

That shut my mate up.

Damen was waiting for us as we exited outside the palace, grinning from ear to ear and not looking bothered by the two extra guests. "You actually showed up."

"Are you surprised?" I asked, smiling back at him. Theon immediately took a step forward, angling himself in front of me.

Damen snorted. "Very. How much convincing did you have to do to get *His Grace* here to agree?"

All my attempts to gently nudge Theon out of the way went ignored, so I stepped around him with a huff, giving him an impatient look. "None? You were happy to come along. Right, honey?"

I gave my mate a teasing look that he didn't return.

"I'm not at all happy to be here," Theon assured me, his gaze so wholly on me that it was as if no one else was here.

"Interesting," Damen murmured. "Well, come on then. We're dining outside—I suppose Allerick thought it would be more neutral ground."

"Yes, the most neutral spot on *his* grounds, surrounded by *his* guards," Theon grumbled, though Wilder—who'd been waiting by the entry room—fell into step behind us. Rainy was quiet, but Xanthia was more than eager to fill the silence, remarking to Damen how much the gardens had changed since the last time she'd been here.

I watched the two of them, trying to work out if there was any weirdness there. Obviously, both she and whoever Damen's mom was had been the former king's lovers at some point. Was it like a polyamory situation? Or maybe more of a one-night stand deal? Shades were a lot less hung up on monogamy than humans were.

"What are you thinking about?" Theon rumbled, dipping his head to speak directly in my ear.

I glanced up at him, surprised he was interested enough to ask. He wasn't exactly the chattiest of dudes from what I'd seen. Then again, he was wildly out of his comfort zone right now—maybe this is what a nervous Theon looked like.

"I'm thinking about your dad's baby mamas and wondering if they're all cool with each other," I admitted.

Theon was silent for a moment. "That isn't what I expected you to say. You never say what I expect you to say."

"Good. Keeps you on your toes."

"The various mothers of all my father's children do get along well, yes," Theon said slowly, like he was translating my question into formal Shade-speak. "He was... very upfront in what his relationship with them would be."

I narrowed my eyes at him. "Is that how you operate? Am I one of many?"

This was totally not the time or place for this conversation, but it had suddenly occurred to me that Theon might also feel the need to spread his seed far and wide, and I would very much *not* be cool with it.

Theon scoffed. "Before you, it had been twenty years since I'd taken a lover."

I made a slightly strangled sound at that. Twenty *years*? "I didn't make you break some sacred vow of celibacy or something, did I?"

"No."

Well, alright then. Apparently, that's all he was willing to say on that subject.

The dinner hadn't been set up too far from the entry room, which seemed like it was a gesture of goodwill for Theon's benefit, and I suspected it was Ophelia's idea.

"Welcome," Allerick said stiffly, standing from the table. Ophelia stood with him, immediately excusing herself from his side to hug me, squealing like we hadn't seen each other in months rather than a couple of days.

"I love your outfit!" Ophelia said, tugging gently at the bow at my neck, just enough to make me nervous. I took a step back under the pretense of admiring her dress, but mostly to put some distance between her and the mark on my neck that I swear everyone could see through my clothes.

As always, Astrid was a lot more cautious, hanging back to eye up Rainy and Xanthia. Tallulah, Meera, and Austin weren't here, so I guessed this was more of an inner circle type dinner, which was cool but also kind of weird to be invited to. Like I was the local school burnout being asked to sit with the popular kids at lunch.

"Verity!" Xanthia called. "Have you met Orabelle?"

"Um, no, I haven't—"

"Come, come," she insisted, beckoning me over to meet the king's mother. I hadn't met her before, but I'd certainly heard of her. Like Theon, she'd objected pretty strongly to feeding from the energy stores. Maybe she still was, since she looked incredibly frail next to Xanthia, and I assumed they were around the same age.

"Orabelle, this is Verity," Xanthia said, presenting me with a flourish. "Isn't she lovely? Look at these beautiful claw decorations. Such a delight!"

"It's nice to meet you," I told her, weighing up the odds of whether I was meant to curtsy or not, and ultimately deciding not to.

Orabelle looked mildly amused by all of Xanthia's gushing. I had *no* idea what to make of it. I hadn't actually done anything to make Xanthia like me. I suspected that she just didn't want Theon to be sad and alone, cooped up in his castle doing... whatever it was he did when he disappeared to "work" all day. Xanthia was the cheerful sort who would have been pleased no matter who I was.

"Shall we sit?" Allerick asked stiffly, gesturing at us to take our seats.

Ophelia dragged me over to sit between her and Astrid, which left a disgruntled Theon sandwiched between Orabelle and Rainy on the opposite side of the table. It was a row of grouchiness, ending with a cheerfully babbling Xanthia on Orabelle's other side, and I shamelessly took advantage of everyone's being busy serving themselves from the platters in the center of the table, to eavesdrop on the conversation happening on the other side.

"So," Orabelle said to Theon, eschewing her goblet of wine for a cup of tea. "I hear you were starving yourself to death."

"I hear we have that in common," Theon countered.

She cackled into her teacup, making everyone else at the table startle. "Who'd have thought we had so much in common, hm, Your Grace?"

Theon gave her a baleful look before taking a healthy swig of his water. Did they know each other? It seemed like they did. Theon was definitely a little older than Allerick.

"Your Hunter is very colorful," Orabelle remarked quietly once everyone else had broken out into smaller conversations. I strained to hear, helping myself to some of the colorful vegetables in the center of the table and wondering idly if they were from Meera's garden.

"She is," Theon agreed.

"Are you fond of her?" Orabelle asked.

I fully anticipated him saying "fuck no with sprinkles on top," or whatever the Theon equivalent of that was, so my expectations were solidly at rock bottom. I wasn't worried that my scent would broadcast any sense of disappointment, because there was zero chance of me feeling any.

Theon eyed Orabelle warily. "Is that a threat?"

"A mere question. Humor me."

I strained to hear over the loud conversation Xanthia was having with Allerick across the length of the table.

"Verity is an excellent... power source," Theon said lamely, not even sounding totally convinced about *that*.

Be still my beating heart. If he kept up that kind of suave dirty talk, the slick would be flowing like water. How was one little power source meant to cope with such effusive praise?

Orabelle snorted. "How very romantic of you to say."

He had the good sense to look a little sheepish, and I gave Orabelle a silent fist bump for that. My feelings weren't hurt—his answer had been a more awkward version of what I'd expected—but Theon was the type of dude that needed to have his feet held to the fire every so often, just to remind him not to go full asshole.

"Verity, did you hear?" Ophelia said, resting a hand on my forearm to draw my attention back into the conversation. "We're doing a royal tour. I've always wanted to see more of the shadow realm, but I really pushed for it after speaking to Austin. He's traveled so much in the short time he's been here. I'm really looking forward to it."

"It's a security nightmare," Astrid muttered, adding more pickles to her plate from the jar she was hoarding. "Soren and I spent all day doing scouting trips for the first few locations. *He* hasn't even visited most of these places before."

"Which isn't good," Ophelia chided, looking across me to her sister. "The court has been far too insular for too long."

I felt Theon's gaze from across the table, finding him being the blatant eavesdropper now. He looked more contemplative than irritated about Ophelia's words, which I was taking as a win. I was going to talk him off this treason ledge if it was the last thing I did.

The topic of conversation moved on to the communication network Astrid was setting up with Austin, and I did my best to focus because I logically knew that this would be an absolute game changer for both realms. Right now, the Hunters controlled the portals on their end, which couldn't stop the Shades from coming and going as they pleased—they just needed darkness to travel—but it was very restrictive for any Hunter deserters who wanted to give life in the shadow realm a whirl. Unless a Shade *happened* to be in the vicinity to whisk them into the in-between, they had no way of traveling there alone right now. The Hunters had closed the portals after a group of us had defected here, so no one could follow in our footsteps.

Unfortunately, my brain wasn't wired to focus on subjects that weren't one-hundred-percent interesting to me, so I tuned out a lot of the finer details.

"We're going to have to do another trip back to see Harlow soon," Astrid was telling Ophelia. "But without Austin. He hates being away from Selene right now, which I get."

I sighed somewhat wistfully at the reminder of Selene's pregnancy. Growing up alone, bouncing around from house to house, and never feeling like I had a family of my own, I'd always dreamed of having children one day. As many as I could handle. I'd been fully prepared to drive a minibus full of car seats and fish-shaped cracker crumbs.

Sebastian had been mostly on board for that too—well, he'd wanted four kids, tops—but after we broke up, I'd put that dream on an indefinite hold, hoping motherhood was still a possibility someday but not staking my entire future on it.

And now I was permanently, *for life*, mated.

What if Theon didn't want kids? This was why you were meant to *talk* to your human lover before you sank your teeth into them. I glared at Theon across the table, hoping I was conveying that with my eyes. He didn't notice.

"How is Selene doing?" I asked.

"Tired, mostly." Ophelia was also smiling dreamily. In contrast, the only time Astrid showed any kind of fear was when the subject of babies came up. "But progressing nicely according to the Shade healers. Obviously, there's an element of the unknown here so she's being monitored pretty closely."

Astrid shuddered, and the captain shot his mate an indulgent grin that she didn't see.

"How go your experiments, Theon?" Damen asked loudly, smirking over the rim of his goblet. "Any success yet?"

Experiments? Was that what his work was?

Had I packed that book on electricity? Maybe my dream wasn't dead yet.

"Plenty," Theon replied coolly.

"Oh? Anything you'd like to show us?" Damen was needling, and I couldn't tell if it was affectionate younger sibling ribbing or something more sinister. The Damen I knew—and I didn't, not really—wasn't malicious.

"You?" Theon asked. "No."

I snorted into my goblet, drawing the attention of the entire table. "What? He's funny."

Not intentionally, but it still counted.

"You're just so *adorable!*" Xanthia squealed. "Such a perfectly complementary pair."

Theon and I probably did seem very in sync as we exchanged disbelieving looks across the table. Look at us, having couple-y reactions. Weren't we just the cutest little power source and power sucker to ever be?

Allerick cleared his throat. "The two of you seem to be getting along well?" he asked uncomfortably, looking at me.

"Very well." I shot him a beaming smile before turning my attention to Theon. "Isn't that right, pookie? You're already so *fond* of me."

Theon stared at me, shifting awkwardly in his seat, and there was a split second of silence before Orabelle cackled. "Oh, I like you. You're fun."

"That's an impressive feat. She sure as shit doesn't like me," Astrid mumbled under her breath.

Allerick looked like he couldn't decide whether he needed to be worried or not, and I kicked Theon lightly under the table, tilting my head at his brother. It wasn't just fun and games now. We were *actually* mated, and if I got dragged to the palace because he wasn't convincingly not an asshole to me, we might *actually* suffer. I didn't know that for sure, but the way the bond directed me to him like Theon was my true north made me think it'd be a real bitch to live with if he wasn't around.

"I am not giving Verity up," Theon said to Allerick, in a voice that dared him to disagree.

Don't be weird, I instructed my pheromones firmly, sensing them getting ready to break into a happy dance.

"No one asked you to," Allerick replied, leaning back in his chair and watching Theon closely. Theon stared right back, but it wasn't with the quiet contemplation Allerick was studying him with.

The look in Theon's eyes reminded me a lot of Pepper, a border collie who used to come into Furocious with her owner and tried to herd whatever other animals were in the store with her fierce collie stare. When faced with beasts triple their size, collies didn't back down, they went to *work*, and that was exactly how Theon seemed to react to pressure.

It was in stark contrast to Allerick—who had the calm protectiveness and stranger-danger instincts of a bullmastiff—or Damen, who had big husky energy.

I glanced at Soren, whose attention alternated between the table and our surroundings, never looking quite at rest. German shepherd, for sure.

"You okay?" Ophelia asked, nudging me gently with her shoulder.

I blinked at her. "Sure. Just thinking about dogs."

"Fair enough." This is why I found her the easiest to get along with—Ophelia was great at rolling with the punches.

Dinner rolled into dessert, and everyone seemed to be making a conscious effort to keep the conversation light after the awkward stare-off.

"Are you going along on the royal tour?" I asked Damen, leaning forward slightly so I could see him at the other end of the table.

"Apparently." If Shades could roll their eyes, he would have.

"Is that such a hardship for you, brother?" Allerick drawled, unimpressed. "Are we interrupting your busy schedule?"

Damen looked slightly chastened, grumbling out a disagreement. I didn't know shit about how this whole system of leadership worked, but it *seemed* like Damen hadn't quite found his role within it.

"While we're all here, I would like to discuss this ban on feeding in the human realm, and my desire for an exemption," Rainy announced, seeing an opening in the conversation and really launching herself straight into it. I couldn't help but admire her confidence—Rainy had more in her teenage years than I had in my thirties.

Theon scoffed. "That's our cue to leave. Come along, Verity."

"No need," Xanthia replied hastily, standing and gesturing for Rainy to do the same. "You young folk stay, enjoy your evening. I will take Rainy home with me."

"Mother—" she objected.

"You don't want to embarrass me in front of my dear friend, Orabelle, do you? My dear, dear friend who I *so* seldom see," Xanthia added innocently, laying on the thickest layer of maternal guilt I'd ever seen.

"But I haven't had a chance to speak to the king yet," Rainy objected furiously, stomping her foot as she stood.

"Oh well. Next time," Xanthia replied cheerfully, already dragging Rainy away. "Bye all!"

I barely stifled a laugh, not wanting to antagonize the tiny tyrant any more than I already had while her mother carted her away, quietly lecturing her the entire way. Theon watched impassively, not looking surprised in the least by his sister's reaction.

"How mad is she going to be later?" I asked him, grinning across the table.

"Probably no more than usual," Theon replied dryly. I snorted before falling silent, noticing that the rest of the table was watching us, scrutinizing our interaction a little too intently for my liking.

They all stared at Theon and me like they were waiting for some big disaster to unfold, and while, *sure*, we were sort of on track for disaster with the secret mark beneath my clothes, I was still a little salty about it. Nobody had watched the other Shade/ex-Hunter pairings like that.

I was probably a little hypersensitive on this front. I'd spent my entire life being looked at like I was the odd one out, and I was kind of over it. It wasn't like these guys hadn't experienced bumps in the road in *their* relationships.

Different bumps to the teeth-shaped one I was hiding under my jumpsuit, but bumps nonetheless.

I'd have stewed over it a little more, but Theon had his glower out in full force, and I didn't trust the next words to come out of his mouth not to set us back several steps in everyone's eyes. The light mood was gone, and it was probably best to call it now and end on a relative high.

"Ready to go, honeybunch?" I asked, shooting him my most syrupy sweet smile across the table.

His agitation cleared, his expression returning to its neutral state of bored arrogance as he turned his attention to me. It wasn't unlike Allerick's default expression, in all honesty. There were more brotherly similarities than I'd realized at first glance.

"Yes."

"You're leaving already?" Ophelia asked as I stood, looking up at me with puppy dog eyes that were probably the sole reason this royal tour was happening.

Ophelia was definitely a golden retriever.

"We are. This has been so fun, though. Thank you for having us."

I hugged all the people I needed to hug, thanked our hosts, and all in all, was a perfectly gracious guest, while my secret mate brooded in the background next to Wilder, waiting for me to finish with the niceties.

The moment we were in the in-between, Theon tucked my hand into the crook of his arm in a very determined way—not so much as a gesture of affection but more like the way you'd tell a rambunctious kid that they had to keep one hand on the cart at the grocery store to stop them from running away.

"That was fun, right?" I asked, peering up at him in the darkness, barely making out the faintest shape of his horns.

Theon grunted.

"I knew you'd have fun."

"I didn't say that."

"I can read between the lines," I assured him, patting his forearm.

Theon huffed quietly, and I chose to interpret it as amusement.

CHAPTER 9

D o you need to feed?" Verity asked as soon as we stepped out of the entry room, Wilder vanishing ahead in front of us to open the door.

Did I *need* to? Objectively, I did not.

Did I *want* to? My shadows shifted restlessly of their own accord, giving away my enthusiasm. Perhaps my twenty years of celibacy had been a mistake. My obvious eagerness was immensely embarrassing.

The corners of Verity's turned up in a smile that seemed almost challenging, as though the events of this evening hadn't already been immensely disruptive to the view I'd formed of her.

"What's in here?" she asked airily, skipping past me to a small, dusty receiving room off the foyer that hadn't been used in years.

Somewhat baffled, I followed her in, startled when she pushed the door shut behind me. Did she *want* to feed me? Or perhaps this was her way of demanding her own pleasure? I certainly had no objection to giving it to her.

Verity came around in front of me, her eyes sparkling with what seemed to be amusement. She was so much more... complex, than I originally thought. Layered. It made things very inconvenient for me.

"Are you going to drop those shadows for me, handsome?"

My shadows fell away, exposing my already hard cock, aching for her attention. Verity's eyes dropped to it, her already sweet scent turning syrupy with desire. From looking at me? The idea seemed absurd.

"I've always wanted to try this," she muttered to herself before shooting me a seductive grin. "Tell me if I do anything you don't like."

And then she dropped to her knees.

Before I could ask *what* it was that she wanted to try, Verity's clawless fingers wrapped around the base of my cock, squeezing where my knot would swell before moving up my shaft. She wished to service me with her hands?

The sensation was certainly pleasant enough. And only a small trickle of power was passing between us, which seemed sensible. I would be very displeased if I accidentally killed my Hunter by taking too much from her.

I startled as Verity leaned forward, pink tongue darting out to lick the tip of my cock. I grabbed blindly for the back of the closest chair, my claws sinking into the upholstery. Verity leaned back on her heels, running her tongue over her blunt teeth with a wink as though to remind me how harmless her enchanting mouth was.

Then she leaned forward, parted her lips, and took my entire cockhead into her mouth. The sound of shredding fabric filled the room as my claws demolished the back of the chair. The hot, wet, sucking sensation of Verity's mouth was almost too much to bear. I was going to humiliate myself instantly.

I sucked in a rasping breath, attempting to bring myself under control, but the moment Verity's hands began moving up and down my shaft again, all hope was lost.

"I won't... I can't..." I gasped out, my vision going hazy at the edges. What sorcery was this? Verity hummed, attempting to take me deeper in her mouth, though my size was limiting her.

With just a few pumps of her delicate hands and the perfect suck of her delectable mouth, I was done for. I attempted to pull back, but Verity kept me in place, squeezing as my knot swelled, massaging it with her fingers as my cum filled her mouth. Some, she swallowed. Some overflowed, running down her chin, willingly painting her skin with my desire.

I'd never seen anything so tempting in all my life.

Verity pulled back, swiping at the cum on her chin with her thumb and licking it clean. I doubled over slightly at the acute wave of desire it sent through me. A strange sound rumbled out of my chest, stuttering to a stop as I straightened in panic.

"You purred for me," Verity said, looking at me in wonder as she climbed to her feet. "No one has ever purred for me before."

I narrowed my eyes, wondering which Shades I needed to kill for not appropriately responding to my mate, before shaking off the errant thought.

"Well, that was fun." Verity bit her lip, wiping more of my cum off her chin. "No wonder you're so fond of me," she added with a wink. "See you tomorrow, pookie."

She patted me on the chest as she passed, letting herself out of the room and heading upstairs, humming cheerfully to herself as she went.

Who was this woman I had tied myself to?

What fools populated Allerick's court that none of them had seen fit to claim her for themselves?

Last night's dinner had altered my perception of Verity, and I was adding that to my mental list of crimes Allerick had committed against me.

In the back of my mind, I'd been certain that Verity was unhappy at the palace and that was why she'd been so content to join me. Or at the very least, that she didn't get along well with the other Hunters who resided there.

But the dinner had proven that wasn't the case.

They *liked* Verity. All of them. She'd been cheerful and charming, and everyone had seemed pleased with her presence.

It had put me in a terrible mood.

I watched from the sitting room on the second story that Aderith had cleared for Verity's use as the two of them walked around the overgrown garden while the rain had briefly ceased, Aderith occasionally pointing at something and Verity leaning in closer to investigate.

I was so absorbed in watching her and the fluid, graceful way she moved that I neglected to scan the perimeter at first. Though once I did, I was out on the balcony and scaling the side of the building before I'd even consciously decided to move.

Who the fuck did Tanix think he was? Monitoring *my* property. Looking at *my* mate.

Possessiveness unlike anything I'd ever experienced before, even for my crown, roared in my veins. Tanix dropped down from the tree on the outskirts of the property he'd been perched in, sprinting for the entry room as though the darkness of the in-between would save him from my wrath.

Wilder was scrambling to follow, though I doubted he even knew what I was chasing, and his advanced age was working against him.

"Watch Verity!" I shouted, ushering him away as I dived into the entry room, the door swinging shut behind me.

Tanix was an idiot if he thought I hadn't done my research on him and his band of would-be rebels. I was already well aware that they had set up their latest camp in a rocky, mountainous area of the realm, unpopular with Shades because of its arid climate and difficult terrain.

I wasn't going to let him get that far, though.

The in-between moved and breathed around me, responding to my urgency as I ran through the darkness, leaping on Tanix's escaping form right before he could reach the threshold of the entry room he was aiming for.

"What did you think was going to happen?" I snarled, grabbing a horn so I could wrench his head back, the weight of my body keeping his pinned to the ground. "What did you think I would do when I found you watching her?"

"She's just food!" Tanix wheezed, straining to escape my grip. "Are you really going to punish your own kind, Your Grace?"

I stilled. "Punish you? How optimistic you are. I'm going to kill you."

In one swift movement, I unsheathed the silver poniard I kept secured at my hip beneath my shadows and sank it into the side of Tanix's neck. In the darkness of the in-between, I could only just make out the smoky shadows pouring freely from his wound as his life force seeped out of him. Tugging my blade free, I rolled him roughly onto his back and struck the killing blow into his chest with my dagger, twisting it until shadows were pouring freely from his body. Tanix gave one last gurgle of pain before falling silent, his body disintegrating into nothing. Or perhaps joining the shadows of the ancestors, if one was to believe the old ways. I hoped they told him what an obnoxious little prick he was, if that was the case.

I climbed to my feet, sliding my blade back into its sheath, irritated at the whole inconvenience of the matter.

Allerick should have dealt with the traitors long before now, or at least sent his surly captain to do the job. But, alas, he'd never bothered, and now it had become my problem.

No one had any respect for my time.

I immediately returned to my own chambers to wash before making for the sitting room in time to meet Verity for our midday meal.

She was already there waiting for me, lounging back in the chair in another floaty pink dress and oddly sparkly boots, and smelling like the most tempting thing I'd ever encountered. I didn't know how I'd managed to leave her alone last night. It had been a true testament to my self-control that I hadn't snatched her from her bed and demanded her attention.

Verity hummed to herself as she sipped her tea, vaguely acknowledging my arrival with a half smile before returning to watching the rain falling outside the window once more.

"How did you spend your time in the human realm?" I asked, more acutely aware now than ever that Verity was, in fact, an individual, rather than just a power source that I had marked and claimed as my own. It made everything far more complicated in my own head.

Perhaps... perhaps biting her without discussing it first had been inappropriate?

No, that was a ludicrous notion. What if I hadn't claimed her for my own? She may have ended up with someone else, and I'd have had to kill them.

"Like what did I do for work?" Verity looked at me over the rim of her cup, her dark eyes assessing and mischievous all at once. "I was an intrepid explorer. I traveled the globe, survived storms, and had park benches named after me."

I watched her for a long moment, trying to decide whether or not she was speaking truthfully. I suspected that Verity derived some kind of *amusement* from me, which was an odd experience in itself. No one had ever associated me with humor, not even at my expense.

"And what were you *really?*"

Verity laughed, her scent bright and sweet. "I worked at a pet store. I've always liked animals. They're more straightforward than people."

"What made you want to come to the shadow realm?" I asked gruffly. I needed to find a way to restore the balance back to where it had been before. Verity needed to be an easily compartmentalized presence in my brain. She was too multifaceted now, too variable, too distracting.

I wasn't sure which box to put her in yet, but I'd find one. Her answers would give me the context I needed, and once I'd put her there, that was where she would stay.

"Everything and nothing, I guess," Verity mused, nibbling absently on a strip of meat and staring out of the window. "On a practical level, my rent had just gone up, so I was going to be forced out of my house anyway—we physically couldn't squeeze any more roommates in there. And then, perhaps on a more emotional level, I guess I hoped I'd find some sense of... belonging. Purpose. I don't know, it sounds stupid when I say it out loud."

It didn't. But reassuring her of that wouldn't help me fit her into the Verity-shaped box I was searching for.

"And did you find it?"

Verity hummed, her gaze unfocused as she looked out the window. "Yes and no."

She wiped her fingers delicately on the napkin as I finished eating, our midday meal coming to an end with me no more decided about what to do with this new mate of mine than I had been before.

"Did *you* find it?" Verity asked, cocking her head to the side, a small smile around her mouth as she threw my own question back at me.

"Did I find what?"

"Whatever it was you were looking for out of this conversation."

I grunted, impressed that she'd figured me out. At least one of us was succeeding. "No."

"You're overthinking it," Verity advised, pushing her chair back as she stood. "You had it right when you were speaking to Orabelle. I'm a power source, and you feed from me. If you want to make it fun, then chase me down for it, I do love a hunt." Verity shrugged, as if she hadn't just dropped the most enticing piece of information I'd ever heard in my lap. "What we have is practical—I get to stay here, build a home for myself here. You get to feed. It doesn't need to be any deeper than that."

She walked away, glancing at me over her shoulder as she pulled the door open. "We should probably talk about kids at some point though. I'd really like a lot of babies. Something to think about."

My fist was wrapped around my cock before she'd shut the door behind her.

CHAPTER 10

F ester," I called softly, trying not to draw attention to the fact that my cat had escaped the confines of my room again until I absolutely had to. I'd been strutting around the palace all afternoon, sassy and confident after my mic-drop moment at lunch, and my goddamn cat was single-handedly undoing all of my hard work. "Where are you?"

I tiptoed as best I could in my knock-off glittery Docs, peeking into every room on the second floor that had a door so much as cracked open. Which wasn't many, to be honest. There was a thin layer of dust on most of them that suggested they hadn't been opened in a while.

What was the point of having such a big house if you didn't use it?

If this was my house—*properly* mine, not this weird, in-between situation I was currently in—I'd have a dedicated room for everything. Reading room. Plant room. Yoga room. Sex dungeon. Nail studio. And it would all be aesthetic as fuck. Having a mansion was totally wasted on Theon.

Maybe I could convince him of the benefits. He was clearly feeling at a loss for what to do with me.

"Fester. Where are you, my favorite boy? Come here, Mommy swears she's not going to be fucking furious at you for stressing her out like this," I singsonged. Not even a single yowl, and I knew that furry little bastard could hear me.

Of course, he could have gone outside, but I'd yet to see an open door or window that led out there—probably because of the incessant rainfall—and it wouldn't be like Fester to run away. Ever since I'd rescued him, he'd been pretty well glued to my hip.

Right before I could start panicking, Fester darted up the stairs from the first floor, sprinting past me with a piece of meat in his mouth that was nearly as big as his head.

"You are a little shit weasel," I whispered, herding him back into my room while he greedily hoarded his prize, leaping onto the ledge with it. "You're in big trouble, mister. I am seriously disappointed in you."

Fester flicked his tail like I was being the annoying one here, chewing loudly on the slice of meat he'd thieved from... somewhere. Presumably, there was a kitchen somewhere. Fester had managed more exploring than I had.

"I'm going to keep looking around, but when I get back, you can expect a lecture on the dangers of sneaking out, young man. Do I make myself clear?"

Fester didn't even deign to yowl at me, far too interested in his snack. I'd taken him into the dining room a couple of times now, and I'd been planning on finding another room today where he could explore before opening up the entire house for his perusal, but apparently, he'd gotten bored with my leisurely timeline.

I shut the storage dungeon door—triple-checking it was all-the-way closed this time—before heading off down the hallway at a less stressed-out pace this time.

Aderith had shown me a small sitting room with a balcony that I'd been making use of, but she hadn't volunteered to give me more of a tour than that, and I hadn't asked. But surely I was allowed to poke around a little on my own? Theon had put a ring on it—and by ring, I meant scary fuck-off-looking bite mark on my neck—so surely I was allowed to wander as I pleased? He'd offered me a whole wing of the house for Fester in the heat of the moment too, I just hadn't got around to taking him up on it. It was difficult when I only saw him at our scheduled midday meal and he spent most of those staring at me like he could crack open my brain if he just put enough thought into it.

I steered well clear of Rainy's entire corridor, even though she was at her mother's house. If anyone was going to materialize out of thin air and give me that twins-from-The-Shining stare, it was Rainy.

To my disappointment, the entire second floor was just empty, dusty bedrooms. Theon had said this was a palace once, so I guessed all the rooms made sense. There were a billion Shades at the current court, and presumably, they needed somewhere to sleep.

It didn't make for the most interesting exploring, though I did note that almost all of the rooms were larger and grander than mine. Mine didn't have rooms on either side though, just the secret staircase that led up to Theon's private room. I guessed the mistress dungeon had been designed with discretion rather than grandeur in mind.

Maybe I could clean a couple of these rooms and invite Tallulah and Meera to stay if they ever wanted a break from Elverston House? If I could convince Theon to rein in the treasonous thoughts around company, we could totally have guests. On reflection, he'd mostly behaved himself at the dinner party. He hadn't said anything about overthrowing Allerick, at least. Clearly, he could read the room when he wanted to.

It was at the end of one corridor, while I was admiring a bust of what appeared to be a previous monarch, sculpted out of what looked like onyx, that I realized I was being followed. There wasn't even the faintest hint of a sound behind me, no brush of air, or a scent to give it away. I just knew. I could *feel* it in the center of my chest. The compass that was the bond to Theon was pointing to him at all times, my new north.

He was close.

"If you want to make it fun, then chase me down for it, I do love a hunt."

Was he taking me up on my challenge? A shiver ran down my spine, apprehension and arousal duking it out for dominance. *You shouldn't be enjoying this*, a voice whispered in my head, sounding eerily like Sebastian's judgmental mother. A voice of quiet condemnation that I hadn't been quite able to shake, reminding me that I was an inherently broken person, even ten years on. *This is wrong.*

But it didn't *feel* wrong. It felt thrilling, and yet safe at the same time. This was Theon. I wasn't in any danger from him—if for no other reason than he needed me to feed.

We could both get what we wanted out of this.

And what I wanted was to be stalked and hunted through the safe confines of the manor walls. I wanted to run. I wanted him to chase me. To pin me down. To *take*.

I could psychoanalyze the *why* of that later.

Or better yet, I could not. I could just enjoy the pleasure and never question it. That sounded way better.

Experimentally, I picked up my pace, the thud of my boots echoing with each step along the corridor. I turned a corner, feeling Theon keep pace with me. My heart pounded a little faster in my chest as I started properly power walking before eventually breaking into a light jog. There were stairs up ahead, and I made a beeline for them, heading up to the third floor.

Something brushed the back of my legs, and I let out a muffled shriek, stumbling slightly on the top step before breaking into a run, narrowly avoiding a plinth with a heavy-looking vase balanced precariously on top.

The gusset of my panties was sticking to my skin, slick dripping out of me at the most rapid rate it ever had.

Catch me, I chanted in my head. *Catch me, catch me, catch me.*

I turned one corner, then another, finding myself in front of a heavy door I didn't recognize. Since the only other option was to turn around and go back, I pressed the handle down and threw my shoulder against it, hefting it open one creak at a time.

It was a library, though it didn't look as though it got much use. The tall outer walls were lined with shelves, and there were lower ones in rows along the middle of the room, occasionally interspersed with heavy writing desks or grand leather armchairs. I crept between the rows, peering over the low gaps in the shelves.

The door didn't open.

My heart was thudding like a bass drum in my chest, drowned out only by my woeful attempts at breathing quietly.

Had I imagined this whole thing? It would be *so* on-brand for me to work myself into a horny lather over a newfound hunting fantasy, only to be running around the corridors by myself like a lunatic.

Worst case scenario, I had a pastel pink merman dildo with a suction base that I hadn't had a chance to try out yet. I was plenty lubed up for it now.

The pull in my chest hadn't eased, though.

I crept through the rows of shelves, peeking over the tops of books and checking behind me every couple of seconds. It was *so* quiet. The bond said he was close, but he couldn't possibly be in this room—

Something wrapped around my ankles and before I could scream, a clawed hand slammed over my mouth, yanking me back against a hard body. I grabbed Theon's wrist instinctively, tugging at him to release me, writhing in his unbreakable grip.

"Settle," he drawled, the pure arrogance in his voice setting my nerves alight. "If you want me to release you, to leave this room and let you continue your afternoon undisturbed, squeeze my wrist three times."

My fingers stilled. Fuck no, I didn't want that. This was the most excitement I'd had in days. Possibly years.

Possibly ever.

Theon hummed, claws dragging over the thin fabric of my dress. I frowned, testing the binds on my ankles that I couldn't see. What *was* that?

"Squeeze once if you wanted me to chase you."

Squeeze.

"Squeeze once if slick is dripping down your thighs."

Squeeze. My face burned with embarrassment, but I had no doubt that he already knew. I'd probably been wafting horny pheromones through the whole manor.

"What a greedy little captive you are." Effortlessly, Theon lifted me with one arm banded around my waist and carried me over to one of the sturdy wooden tables. "Three squeezes if you want me to stop. Now are you going to bend over or do I have to *make* you bend over?"

I didn't bend over.

I didn't squeeze either.

There was a sudden rush behind me, like air whooshing past, and suddenly I was even more *caught*. Bound around the ankles, around the wrists that were dragged down so my palms were on the table, around my waist.

Theon's hands dragged up the back of my thighs, pushing my dress up over my hips and freeing my mouth.

"What is that?" I gasped, though I was pretty sure I already knew.

"I have shadows to spare, little captive. Shadows for playing with you. Whatever I expend now, I'm confident you will restore." His shadows squeezed my wrists and ankles a little tighter, just to show me he could.

Tentacles. It had to be tentacles.

Sexy as fuck, endlessly adaptable shadow tentacles.

The possibilities were endless.

I whimpered my way through a weak, embarrassingly eager orgasm, pussy clenching desperately around nothing.

"You like them," Theon murmured, sounding surprised. They flexed around me again and I leaned into them, pressing my ass back against his thick, hard cock.

"I fucking love them."

Theon hesitated for a moment.

"You're still my prisoner," he reminded me sternly, though I suspected it was more for his own benefit. Evidently, his takeaway from our lunchtime conversation was that he should double down.

"Mmhm, that's right. I've been your prisoner from the moment I *volunteered* to come here. You're a very big, bad duke keeping the poor defenseless little huntress imprisoned in your evil lair."

"Yes. You *are* imprisoned here," he reiterated, clearly debating whether or not I was mocking him.

"And I've been a very naughty little prisoner. You should probably punish me." I giggled at my tragic attempt at dirty talk, bending over further so my breasts pressed against the tabletop.

"I *will* punish you. I am in control here."

I grinned against the table. He was adorable. It blew my mind that no one else seemed to realize that, or Theon would have been a proper court celebrity.

"Go on then. Show me what those tentacles can do."

"Tentacles," Theon repeated slowly, trying out the word before seemingly deciding he liked it. "They can do anything I like. They're extensions of me."

I almost came again. Theon's nose was pressed to my shoulder, inhaling deeply, a drop of his saliva sliding down my back.

"You're hungry, Your Grace," I purred, wanting to make him as weak as he made me. "Let me feed you. I'm your captive. Your meal. Take from me. *Use* me."

My clothes were in ribbons, shredded by his claws before I'd even realized he was going to undress me.

Teeth dragged down my back, the shadows pinning me in place so that he could explore to his heart's content. He nipped at my ass just enough to sting before shoving my thighs wider, throwing me off-balance so I was mostly lying on the table.

I stiffened as sharp claws caught my pussy lips, dragging them apart. Theon's thumbs scraped gently over my sensitive flesh, not enough to slice me open, but definitely enough to add an edge of fear to my arousal.

"You like this," he murmured approvingly. "Your scent gives you away, even if I couldn't see how slick you are for me. And with such fragile skin." He pressed the tip of one claw in a little, not enough to break the skin, and I sucked in a breath. "Most Shade females wouldn't even allow this."

"Not super in the mood to hear about them right now," I snapped, though my ire was quickly forgotten when he returned his claws to the slightly safer perch of my labia and replaced them with his tongue running through my folds.

He didn't bother with soft words or reassurances—I doubted he knew how. Theon had probably never comforted anyone in his life.

He was playing my body like an instrument, though, so I couldn't really find it in myself to be mad. The binds around me tightened every time I tried to squirm, and I loved how *contained* I felt. Perhaps it was wrong that it made me feel safe, but that was the effect it had.

"Let me taste one," I begged, attempting to fuck myself back on his rough tongue.

"Taste what?" he asked, voice muffled by my pussy.

"A tentacle." Wasn't that obvious?

I found myself on my back, landing with a gentle *oof* as Theon's tentacles rolled me, boosting me fully onto the table. The binds around my ankles shoved my legs up, my toes at the very edge of the surface, entirely exposed to the monster rising slowly from the floor where he'd been kneeling, glowing pink eyes trained intently on me.

"Open."

My mouth opened instantly. Another tentacle appeared, unfurling from Theon's hip and snaking its way toward me.

"Thicker," I rasped, watching it in a trance.

"You'll take what I give you."

Or that. That sounded good, too.

The first brush of his shadows against my tongue was cool, the texture an odd mixture of light and solid. It *felt* like it should dissolve like cotton candy, but it seemed to go the other way, growing thicker instead. It didn't really taste like anything, which wasn't a bad thing. It made it easier to focus on the sensation of it slowly crawling over my tongue toward the back of my throat.

Theon climbed over my body, resting one finger over my open palm as he braced himself on the desk. "Squeeze three times if you want me to stop," he reminded me.

So polite.

"Squeeze once if you want more."

I immediately squeezed once, and my heart did a tiny little flutter at the delay, as he waited to see if any more would come. He may *act* like a raging psychopath, but there was a kind soul underneath all that bluster and treason; I was sure of it.

Shadows poured down my throat, and my eyes watered slightly at the sudden fullness, but *fuck*. It was even better than I'd imagined. Theon lowered his body, grinding his cock against my aching clit, and I let out a needy whine, begging him without words to fuck me. I wanted to feel him everywhere. I wanted to be surrounded and filled and owned by him, all at once.

Without any preamble, he thrust the full length of his cock into me, only the tight grip he had on my limbs stopping me from flying up the table. I let out a garbled yell around a throatful of shadows, my eyes rolling back in my head.

"Why do you make me feel this way?" Theon growled in my ear, fucking me at an almost punishing rate. "Like I'm losing my mind."

I doubted he would have wanted an answer anyway, not that I was in any state to give him one. I gagged slightly on the increasingly thick tentacle, and he immediately eased off, the massaging, undulating movements almost relaxing compared to the brutal thrusts of his cock.

The contrast between rough and gentle was intoxicating, and I came almost instantly, clenching around his cock in an orgasm that rolled immediately into another. Slick pooled on the table beneath me, dripping off the edge onto the stone floor in a series of quiet *plinks*. The smell of sex replaced the musty scent of the closed-up library. I'd never be able to think about books again without remembering how it felt to be stuffed full of Theon's cock and shadows.

He muttered a string of curses under his breath, his movements growing more labored as he pushed his burgeoning knot in, grunting in exertion to get it fully into place as his own orgasm ripped through him. I let out a muffled groan as his knot expanded, lodging itself firmly inside me, rubbing my oversensitized inner walls in a way that straddled the line between 'too much' and 'just right.'

I'd never felt so thoroughly consumed by someone in my life, and it was equal parts liberating and terrifying. More frightening than the bite mark on my neck and the mate bond in my chest, was the way Theon made me feel.

Like no form of indulgence was out of reach.

Like my pleasure was his to command.

Like in all the limited ways I sought out happiness for myself in this life, he'd be able to provide it.

The tentacle in my mouth withdrew, and I panted my way through seemingly endless waves of pleasure, my pussy stretched tight around his bulbous knot.

For a long while, there was no speaking. I could barely muster the energy to breathe, let alone to talk.

I also wasn't entirely sure what to say after something that intense. Based on our first foray into feeding, Theon didn't *do* cuddles. Probably best to wait in silence until his knot softened and then we could both get on with our days.

"You enjoyed that," Theon rasped, though it sounded sort of like he was confirming rather than accusing.

"Very much."

He harrumphed grumpily, though I was familiar enough with his drama queen ways now not to take it personally.

"What about you?" I asked, verifying that I hadn't taken advantage of him.

"Yes." Verbose as always. He paused for a moment before speaking again. "What else can I do to you?"

It might have been the most romantic thing anyone had ever said to me.

I took a deep breath, and let every fantasy I'd ever had spill out.

CHAPTER 11

derith was all but glowing, presumably having fed from the mostly unused stores here in the manor that I'd been topping up with excess power I'd gathered from feeding from my mate.

Despite how liberally I'd siphoned—both Aderith and Wilder were comfortably old enough to be feeding from the stores regardless of the current situation—I felt no weaker. Siphoning had merely been enough to take the jittery edge off.

Everyone deserved to feel this level of full. Aches and pains I didn't know I had disappeared. My eyes glowed brighter, my skin felt smoother, even my claws and teeth felt stronger.

Eschewing my workshop, I instead headed upstairs, toward the turret that rounded off the western corner of the manor. The circular study at the top of the tower afforded some of the best views of the expansive forest that surrounded my home, and everything about the room and its aspect were meant to inspire a sense of awe. This was the place where I should be taking meetings—in my spot behind the grand wooden desk, currently covered in dust, with a great fire roaring in the currently empty grate. My father had certainly done as much when he'd resided here.

I'd never had much cause to use it.

My workshop had always been the place that had called to me most. I preferred to be practical, to use my intelligence to *create* rather than to theorize. But in the case of the Hunters, drawing up theoretical plans was an unavoidable reality. I suspected efficiencies could be made to the stores and the siphoning process, and I certainly intended to investigate that further, but ultimately, we needed more Hunters in the shadow realm. It was a question of numbers before anything else.

I pulled out a fresh sheaf of paper, a pen, and an ink pot, considering what I knew of the situation, and now knew of Verity.

She'd wanted a sense of purpose—a very natural thing for any sentient being to want. I had been... not as aware as I should have been about the Hunters having deep emotional needs of their own, but I wouldn't overlook that aspect again.

Large-scale food production was going to be a key component. Verity had favored the brightly colored selection of items at the dinner party. More would be needed to provide for a greater number of humans, and that would also create opportunities for work—both for Hunters and for Shades. I spread my map of the realm out on my desk, making a note on the paper of locations which I thought would be suitable, based on what I'd seen of food production in the human realm. The crops grown in the shadow realm were primarily used to feed the livestock—surely, some of those pastures could be mixed use?

They would also need accommodation. I'd only seen the outside of Elverston House, but I couldn't fathom how Allerick thought that was a suitable place to host honored guests. However, their proximity to the palace and the Guards' barracks was advantageous, especially when they were new to the realm and adjusting.

With a huff of irritation at keeping any part of Allerick's "plan" intact, I quickly sketched the outside of Elverston House as I remembered it, noting down the repairs I could recall off the top of my head, as well as a few additional features that could be added on to make the place more functional. Certainly, clearing some of the vegetation on the border would be wise, allowing room for a pergola perhaps, somewhere that Hunters and Shades could meet that offered *some* privacy, but in a public environment for safety.

Setting that aside, I drafted a list of human-friendly forms of employment here in the shadow realm, noting down the sort of lifestyle they afforded. Not all of them would wish to sit in the confines of the palace all day, waiting around for something to happen *to* them. Some would want to be masters of their own fate.

Absurd that Allerick hadn't considered such a thing, but I wasn't surprised. With a slight frisson of uneasiness, I realized that perhaps if I were in his position, I wouldn't have either.

After all, Allerick's fate had been determined for him from a young age, and the life of a monarch involved a *lot* of sitting around, waiting for things to happen. Of course, leadership was required, but there was an entire council to assist him, as well as other figures of authority, responsible for their own spheres, such as Captain Soren.

Allerick had a high level of responsibility, but a low level of daily routine, and not everyone would be content to operate as such.

With the few minutes I had before I was due downstairs to meet Verity for lunch, I drafted suggestions for protective laws that would enshrine the rights of Hunters who pledged their allegiance to the shadow realm. Slightly less contentedly, I suggested a list of appropriate punishments for Shades who broke the rules, uneasily thinking of my own situation.

No, that was ridiculous.

It wasn't the same at all.

My actions had *improved* Verity's life here in the shadow realm. The end justified the means.

Swallowing thickly, I finished my list of proposed punishments and made my way downstairs to the dining room. I bypassed the door, following the pull of the mating bond down to the first floor and along the corridor that led to the kitchens.

I hovered outside the archway while Verity spoke to Wilder, seemingly unaware of my presence.

"Did there used to be parties here?" Verity was asking him. "Like balls and such?"

"Not in my time," Wilder laughed, making me startle. Since when did he know how to laugh? "But back when this was a functioning palace, yes. Of course. There is a ballroom on this level, though it's been closed up for many decades now."

Verity hummed. She made such pleasant, soothing sounds. "What a waste. Surely, some of these rooms could be opened up again? I wouldn't mind cleaning them."

"I'm sure His Grace wouldn't be opposed to taking on more staff for such a task," Wilder replied, sounding vaguely horrified at the notion of Verity scrubbing dusty floors herself.

"Oh no, that would defy the point. I want something to do." Her voice was changing in pitch, as though she was moving around the kitchen. "Shall I bring these dishes upstairs?"

"Really, I can do that—"

"That's okay, Theon can help me carry them, he's hovering in the corridor like a weirdo."

Ah, I hadn't been as discreet as I'd thought. I had to give my little mate credit, nothing in her tone had given away her awareness of my presence. Her easy charm and unflappable nature would serve her well when she was crowned queen at my side someday.

CHAPTER 12

Hey," I said, pulling Aderith aside after breakfast. "Could I have some cleaning supplies?"

She looked ready to pass out on the spot, which was an even more dramatic response than Wilder's look of horror in the kitchen yesterday.

"I just thought I'd spruce up the library a little. It's such a nice spot, and even though I can't read any of the books, I've been enjoying looking at the illustrations—"

"I will clean it, Your Grace," Aderith said hurriedly, fidgeting uncomfortably. "That is my role."

"No, please, I really want something to occupy my time," I insisted.

She fidgeted again. "Well, okay. If you're certain."

"I am."

"The only reason I haven't maintained it is that His Grace closed up most of the rooms to reduce my workload."

"Of course, that makes total sense," I reassured her, not wanting to think I was criticizing her. "And it also makes sense that if I'm the one opening those rooms up, then I should be the one to take care of them. Deal?"

I smiled, but it didn't seem to ease her mind any. Theon walked past at that moment, heading down to his basement man cave to do... whatever he did all day.

"Honeycakes," I called out sweetly, reveling in his sigh of irritation. "Would you mind terribly if I cleaned the library?"

He shot me a disgruntled look, probably at the term of endearment, already slinking down the stairs. "No."

"Well, there we go. It's settled."

Aderith still looked vaguely disgruntled as she led me to a cleaning closet, and I grabbed whatever was within reach before scurrying upstairs to the library, not wanting to make her any more uncomfortable than she already was. Clearly, I was disrupting the order of things here, and I felt pretty bad about that.

But I also had a short attention span and as soon as I was absorbed in my task, I forgot about Aderith entirely. The leather-bound books on the shelves were caked in dust, and I'd wrapped a scarf around the lower half of my face to minimize how much of it I inhaled, but it was totally worth it because the job of cleaning them was incredibly rewarding. Beneath the years of neglect were beautifully engraved covers, some shimmering with silver foil, and I carefully rubbed at the surfaces with a dry cloth, getting into all the crevices until they came up looking shiny and new. Well, maybe not new. Maybe just less ancient.

There were hundreds of books in this library at least, and it was probably going to take me several years to get through the entire room. But what else did I have going on? Maybe getting this manor back to its former grandeur would be my newfound purpose.

Besides, there was something kind of symbolic in it. The manor was interesting and grand and beautiful, but it had been neglected and shut away for a long time. Much like its owner.

Okay, maybe I was romanticizing Theon a little too much. At least some of his neglect seemed to be self-inflicted. Sure, Damen was pretty antagonizing when it came to Theon, but I didn't think he'd have actually objected if Allerick had insisted on having Theon around more. The tension between the two older brothers had definitely been evident at that dinner, but it didn't seem like a simple matter of Allerick banning Theon and that was that. I was pretty sure they'd *both* been avoiding each other.

Maybe I could be a positive influence by helping Theon build bridges with his brothers?

Honestly, aside from feeding Theon, what was I bringing to the table? He'd indulged me in my chase fantasy and had let his tentacles float free ever since I said I liked them. I really needed to up my game.

"What are you doing?"

I shrieked at the sound of Rainy's flat voice, dropping the book I'd been holding with a thud, and clutching my frantically beating heart.

"Oh my god, wear a bell or something. You just took ten years off my life."

If anything, Rainy looked thrilled at that pronouncement, the little shit. I wasn't all that mad. I'd been an asshole little teenager who thought I knew everything once too.

"You smell incredibly bad," she said bluntly.

I shot her a dark look, tugging my scarf down under my chin. "You gave me a fright. Hunter fear is a very pungent smell, or so I'm told."

Rainy harrumphed, dropping down to sit on the floor opposite me and watching in silence as I picked up the book and resumed cleaning.

"Got bored at your mom's house?" I asked after the quiet stretched for an uncomfortably long time.

"She always wants to spend time with me," Rainy replied, as though this was a terrible burden she was being forced to bear.

"Presumably, because she loves you and misses you when you're gone," I pointed out mildly, hoping she wouldn't gut me with her scary claws. Who knew how teenage angst manifested in Shades.

Rainy shifted uncomfortably. "Yes, well, I'm not an infant any longer. I don't need to be coddled by my mother."

I ducked my head to hide a smile. "I'm much older than you, and I'd love to be coddled by my mother."

"Does she hate you because you came here?" Rainy asked bluntly.

"She's dead."

There was a long pause. "That's probably better than hating you right?"

A startled laugh escaped me at the breathtakingly inappropriate question. "I've never given it much thought."

"My mother is a bit annoying, but I don't think I'd like it if she hated me," Rainy declared, glaring at me as though daring me to disagree. I honestly had no idea why she was here. Were we bonding? Was she trying to decide how to kill me and get away with it? I needed a little more information to go on.

"Well, I don't think you're at any risk of that. Your mother adores you."

More awkward silence. I set aside the book I'd been working on, picking up the next one in the pile.

"My brother likes you," Rainy said suddenly. I couldn't tell if it was an observation or an accusation.

"You think so?" I asked absently. There were definitely a couple of parts of me that Theon liked a whole lot, but that wasn't an appropriate conversation to have with a teenager.

"I want to know why." *No, kid, you definitely don't.* "My brother doesn't like anyone except me, Aderith, Wilder, and sometimes, Mother."

"It must be my sparkling personality. Or maybe my sense of humor? You're probably not seeing it yet, but I promise, I'm actually hilarious."

"Even if that's true"—*Rude*—"it wouldn't be reason enough for Theon to like you. He doesn't care for frivolity."

She said the word with such pronounced disgust that I set the book down, looking at her more closely. "Everyone needs a little frivolity in their lives. There's nothing wrong with it, you know. Fun just for the sake of having fun. It's healthy."

"I don't have time for that," Rainy replied primly. "I have to train. I'm going to be stronger than my brother someday." She gave me a speculative look. "You'll have to find somewhere else to live if I overthrow him."

"I'll keep it in mind," I replied wryly.

Wilder slid into the room, making us both jump. He doubled over for a moment to catch his breath, and Rainy stood up, looking *almost* sheepish.

"Your mother is looking for you," Wilder chided, straightening up but slumping slightly against the door frame.

"I'm going, I'm going," Rainy mumbled, trailing after him as he ushered her out of the room without looking back.

Had that gone well? I couldn't tell. Considering how flagrantly rude Rainy had been to me since I'd shown up, I still felt strangely compelled to try make a good impression on her. I mean, we were sisters-in-law for all intents and purposes now, right? There could only be benefits to us having a good relationship.

And if I could introduce a little silliness to both her and Theon's lives, surely that could only be a good thing. Both of them took themselves way too seriously.

Just as I was starting to get hungry, Theon appeared in the library with two plates of food, glancing down irritably as Fester trotted along at his feet. I schooled my expression, though I hadn't expected Theon to come to me. I'd assumed our mandated midday meals *had* to happen in the dining room.

"Your beast is far too fearless," Theon grumbled. "If I don't fiercely guard my plate, it steals the meat straight off it."

"*He*," I corrected primly, standing up and dusting off my tie-dye leggings. "Not *it*. And Fester was abandoned. It took a lot of convincing to get him to trust me—he's mostly chill now, but he still steals food a lot. Naughty Fester," I added, giving him a stern look that he ignored completely, yellow eyes fixed on the plates in Theon's hands.

Theon set the plates down on the table he'd once bent me over, and my face flamed as I dragged a seat over to join him. Was he thinking about that day? He didn't look like it. I wished I had a poker face.

"There is a lingering… *unpleasantness* to your smell," he observed, ever the charmer.

"Your sister was here."

Theon made a grumbling sound. "Wilder said as much. I hope she behaved herself, though my expectations are low."

I waved away his concern. "She was fine. I mean, she gave me a fright, hence the smell. It was good, though. I'd like to get to know her better."

Theon looked doubtful. "Why?"

"Why not?" I shrugged. "I've never had a sister. It could be fun."

He grumbled something under his breath that I didn't quite catch, though it sounded like he said "better than having brothers."

Theon's gaze tracked over the stack of books on the floor I'd been working on, and I somehow felt my skin grow hotter, though I had no idea why. Maybe it was just because I knew that he'd been down in his mad scientist lab doing god-knows-what all morning, and I'd been… dusting book covers.

"You're sure you wouldn't rather have Aderith do this?" Theon asked skeptically. "You're a duchess. You don't have to clean."

"Am I?" I did a double take when I realized there was a sizeable portion of potato on my plate, sliced into thin rounds and fried. Not fried for very long, by the looks of it, but I appreciated the gesture, nonetheless.

"I requested some human food from the palace," Theon said, eyeing the potato warily. "More should arrive within the next few days. And of course you're a duchess. You're my mate."

My stomach did a little somersault at the reminder, even though it was still a shady, on-the-down-low mating and totally didn't count.

"I thought titles were more of a by-marriage thing. And thank you for the food, that was very thoughtful of you."

He grunted in acknowledgment. "We could get married today, but I assume you would be uncomfortable with the idea since *you* want to keep our mating a secret."

"How do you manage to make it sound like I'm being super unreasonable about that?" I laughed. "Did you see the look on everyone's faces when I said I'd go with you? Do not you remember how horrified they were?"

"I was only looking at your face."

"Oh." I blinked. "That's kind of romantic."

Theon narrowed his eyes. "I was merely trying to work out if you were in possession of your full faculties or not."

"That's slightly less romantic."

"I have never claimed to be romantic. Why would you say such a thing?"

I stabbed a piece of semisoft potato with my fork, waving it in his face. "Because you're a sweet, considerate mate who got me potatoes and lets me play with cleaning products? What more could a girl ask for?"

"I suspect you are not being sincere."

I shoved my food in my mouth, doing my best to suppress my smile.

"What have you been working on this morning?" I asked eventually, not really expecting him to answer but valiantly attempting to make small talk anyway. We were a pair now. A unit. A *team*. We'd both be better off once we learned how to talk to one another.

Theon chewed in silence for a moment before wiping his fingers on a napkin. I'd spent a lot of meals with Shades—fancy Shades, supposedly—and Theon ate far more *elegantly* than they did. Like he'd gone to Shade finishing school or something.

"The project I have been working on is giving me some difficulty." He said it like he was appalled that was even a possibility. "This morning, I visited the in-between to harvest some of the substance of it. Sometimes, I find it more productive to work on something else—even if it's something without much tangible use—until a new idea for a solution presents itself to me."

I gaped at him, slightly amazed that he'd volunteered so much information. Usually, he had a one-sentence-at-a-time limit when speaking.

"You harvested... the substance? Of the in-between?" I almost shuddered. The in-between looked like pure, empty darkness to me, but what if it had been filled with, like, fungus or something this whole time, and I'd never noticed?

Theon glanced up from his meal, pinning me with those pretty pink eyes. "Come and see it for yourself after our meal, if you wish."

"In your workshop?" I perked up instantly. "I sort of assumed I wouldn't be allowed in there."

"Why?"

"I don't know. Because it's your space, I guess."

"I have no objection to you entering my workshop, though I would suggest you not touch anything if I'm not there. Some items are more volatile than others."

"Yeah, I'm definitely not going to start poking around in your experiments, you don't have to worry about that," I assured him. There was a warm feeling in my chest that he seemed so completely at ease with me going into his private space. "You can come into my room whenever you like," I added, feeling like I needed to extend an invitation of my own.

Theon hummed noncommittally, and we finished the rest of our meal in comfortable silence, Fester nibbling on the piece of meat I gave him at my feet.

It was nice. Relaxing. Maybe I didn't feel like I'd magically found some deep and meaningful purpose in life, but it kind of felt like I was on the right track. Like a peaceful, happy existence was actually within reach, if we were both brave enough to just reach for it.

CHAPTER 13

Verity chattered about the library as we made our way downstairs to the workshop below the manor. It had originally been the servants' quarters, but I'd moved Aderith and Wilder up to the first floor as the only full-time residents here, and knocked some of the walls down to create a large open space here for me.

"Wow," Verity breathed, pausing at the bottom of the staircase to admire the space. "This is seriously impressive."

It wasn't, particularly. It was a large space, with several fireplaces dotted around—I'd kept those when I'd taken out the walls—and long benches covered in half-finished projects, haphazardly arranged by their level of completion.

There was an odd sensation gnawing at me that I hadn't recalled experiencing since childhood. Self-consciousness, perhaps? What an odd notion. I'd never particularly cared what anyone thought of my experiments before, though I had encountered very few who would offer an opinion on it either way since my fall from grace. No one visited me here. I didn't go out of my way to socialize with anyone.

My mother, sister, and staff already knew where my interests lay.

Perhaps it was Damen's condescending comments from the dinner party pressing heavily on my mind. I wasn't even sure how he *knew* about my hobby. Then again, the manor had once had more staff. I'd slowly let them go over the years.

"Did you make all this stuff?" Verity asked, breaking away from my side to examine something on the bench, keeping her word by carefully not touching anything.

Frankly, I couldn't remember what my plans had been for the thing she was examining from every angle. This end of the bench was a wasteland.

Instead, I headed for the far end of the room where I'd been working earlier, while Verity followed behind me, pausing occasionally to look at things that caught her attention.

It was strangely pleasant to have her in my space. I'd mostly told her she was free to enter this room because everyone else in the household did—it had never been a *secret* space, just one that required some degree of caution.

I picked up the tiny orb of pure darkness from within the small pile of fabric I'd left it in, holding it up to the silvery light to check that it was still as pure and solid as it had been before I'd taken a break for my midday meal. Not a sliver of silver penetrated the thick blackness. What I would *do* with it, I had no idea. But knowing that I *could* harvest and store it was useful knowledge in and of itself.

Verity sidled up next to me, and I lowered the small orb to her eye level, as though showing others my work was something I *ever* did.

"So these are the shadows of the in-between?" she asked, moving closer to peer into the orb. The darkness of the orb was reflected in her brown eyes, and I was so entranced by it that for a long moment, I forgot to respond.

"Yes," I said, my voice oddly raspy. "Though they're not quite shadows. Our word for it is *caspite,* it is more like... living darkness, I suppose. It expands, takes over everything it can."

"Like a weed?"

"I suppose that's as good of an analogy as any. It can't survive in either the human realm or the shadow realm for long."

"Will it survive in here?" Verity asked, running her dainty finger over the smooth glass. She was so distracting with her... gentleness. No one or nothing in my life had ever been as *delicate* as she was, both as a being and in how she treated other things.

"I believe so," I replied belatedly, remembering she'd asked me a question. "It's a compact space. The reason it can't spread into either realm is that there is too much space and too much light, the darkness *dies*, for lack of a better term. It rapidly expands, and before long it's spread too thin and dissipates."

"Is the in-between not a big place then?" Verity frowned, probably thinking back on her own journeys through it.

"It's difficult to explain." My grasp of human languages was excellent, but some concepts were still hard to translate. "You would be better served not thinking of it as a place, but living, malleable, interconnected *matter*. For Shades, folding and adjusting that matter to get to where we want to go is second nature."

For me, the way that Verity's kind navigated the in-between was far stranger than my method.

"And you managed to capture some in this tiny ball?" Verity asked, looking up at me, a small smile playing around her mouth. "You're pretty freaking smart, you know that?"

"Of course I know that."

She grinned. "And what are you planning on doing with it?"

"Nothing in particular."

"You did all that work for nothing?" she asked, her tone slightly disbelieving.

"At this stage, I have no use for it." I gestured at the shelves of half-finished and abandoned projects behind me. "Sometimes, an experiment is just an experiment. An exercise to test the bounds of what is possible. I wanted to see if I *could* capture a minuscule amount of *caspite* and contain it without it spreading, and now I know that I can. Keep it, if you like. A trinket for you."

"Really?" Verity beamed up at me, her eyes lighting up in a most intriguing way. Her scent sweetened, not quite in the way of arousal, but something nearly as tantalizing. Was she so easily pleased? It was very little effort for me to provide her with small gifts like this.

So little effort for a smile that was so very rewarding. *Enchanting*, even. Was it any wonder that I kept losing my head wherever Verity was concerned? Her brightness was so very disorienting.

"Yes, of course. It's yours."

"I wonder if I can attach it to a necklace or something," she murmured, admiring it once more. "It's so cool."

Why hadn't I thought of that? That was far more impressive as far as gifts went.

"Sit," I instructed, gesturing at the bench seat while I crossed over to my metal working station, setting the orb down in a nest of fabric so it didn't roll away. There were piles of silver chains on the bench, mostly remnants of jewelry that I'd found around the manor over the years. Things left by forgetful guests back when this had served as a palace, or items my mother had discarded. She didn't mind—she'd always been very encouraging of my endeavors.

The fire was always going in this room, but I stoked it higher to heat the solder, before hunting through my collection of broken pieces to find something that would suit.

"This is such a next-level man cave," Verity said, picking through the assortment of scrap metal on the table.

"Don't touch that, you'll cut yourself," I chided. "And I'm not a *man*, nor is this a *cave*. It is a workshop."

"Same difference." Her absolute refusal to be afraid of me was disconcerting. Not that I *wanted* her to be afraid of me, necessarily. She just... should have been. "Have you always been into inventing and stuff?"

"Not always. When I was young, I lived at my father's court full-time, training with the expectation of one day inheriting the throne. Allerick is ten years younger than me. It was only as he grew older that I had... time, for such frivolities as this."

"When he showed signs of perhaps becoming king one day?" Verity asked tentatively.

I never talked about it. Everyone in my life knew better than to bring the subject up. And yet, the idea of silencing Verity was untenable.

"Yes. There are signs of a great capacity for power in young children—the ability to 'hold' extensive power without needing to siphon or risk growing ill. The royal line has been cultivated with that great capacity for power in mind. The monarch functions as a power source for much of the realm. Eventually, as was to be expected, Allerick challenged me for my position as heir. Clearly, I lost. He's not *that* much stronger than me," I added, only slightly bitterly.

Given the age difference, I should have won easily. But Allerick had exhibited better restraint in our challenge. Better *control*. I'd lost my temper and burned out by throwing everything I had into it, and he'd been the last one standing.

The shame I felt at my lack of self-control haunted me to this day. That was not something I *ever* discussed.

"Did you have to challenge Damen too?"

I stiffened slightly, busying myself with the solder and the assortment of silver I'd found. "Yes."

I hated even hearing his name on her lips. There was no possible way that Damen didn't want Verity for himself. Damen was unattached, and Verity was too perfect, too vibrant, too interesting for him *not* to want to steal her away for himself.

Why else would *he* be coming here to check on her? It would be far more logical that the captain and his assassin mate perform welfare checks. Verity would be far more comfortable speaking to Astrid than she was speaking to Damen.

"That must have been a difficult time for you," Verity murmured.

I grunted, not wishing to elaborate any further. There had been no place for me in my father's court, or what would eventually become Allerick's court. No one felt it was a loss that I'd lost another place in the succession to Damen—Allerick had grown up with him, already trusted him, and it was a net benefit to everyone that the monarch had an heir they could rely on. I'd been raised here, alone, and no amount of forced proximity could establish that trust between Allerick and me.

"And you've lived here ever since?" Verity asked. I hummed in agreement, fitting together the pieces I needed for the necklace.

"This was originally the home of the court. Later it became the monarch's private residence for many centuries. Their place to go when they wished to escape the scrutiny of court. By the time Allerick was born, my father had changed his mind on where the heir should live, but when I was young, he felt strongly that I should be raised here. This property was given to me for my and my mother's use, with our own staff. Thus far, no one has taken it away from me."

That didn't mean it would never happen, but Allerick seemed inclined to let me keep it so far.

"How come your mom doesn't live here anymore?" Verity asked, a soft smile crossing her face. "I like your mom."

"She likes you too," I mumbled, not entirely sure how I felt about that. Mother had wanted me to find someone because she felt like I was *lonely*, which was an absurd concept. I wasn't lonely. I was fine on my own. "She inherited her own family seat and lives there now. What did your parents think of you coming to the shadow realm?"

Verity made a sound of surprise. "They're dead, didn't I tell you?"

"No." My chest felt strange. "I would have remembered that."

Verity shrugged, looking down at the bench. "It was a long time ago. I was young."

A strange emotion I wasn't used to feeling for anyone other than myself sat heavily in my chest. Sorrow, perhaps.

"That only dulls the pain, it doesn't extinguish it," I said quietly, thinking of my own father's death at the hands of a Hunter in the human realm five years earlier. Our relationship had been strained for the latter part of his life as he focused all of his attentions on Allerick, and to a lesser degree, Damen. I was too old to feel as though I was being replaced, but perhaps feelings weren't always logical.

I missed him. And I was angry at him. It was an ongoing struggle to reconcile the two.

"No, it doesn't." Verity looked wistful. "I've been thinking of my parents a lot lately. Probably because it's always raining here. Whenever it rained, my ma would make *pannekoek*, with cinnamon and sugar. I've been really craving them lately." She shook her head slightly, almost as though she was exasperated with herself.

Verity seemed to have far more patience for everyone except herself. It was very strange, as she was far more tolerable than most everyone else I'd ever encountered.

"Who cared for you as a child?"

"Everyone and no one. The Hunters have their own version of foster care. I guess because they can't ship children who can see monsters other humans can't see out into the general population. Or they could, but we'd be institutionalized pretty quickly. I was usually placed with a family who had similarly aged kids for a while—sometimes weeks, sometimes a couple of years—and I'd stay until I got inconvenient, I guess. No one treated me badly or anything, but I don't think they volunteered to look after me necessarily. The Council just expected them to, and they made the best of it."

"You had no other relatives who could take you?" I asked, an indignant sort of rage crawling up my spine at the idea of a young Verity being dumped on apathetic caregivers, never able to form true attachments with any of them.

"My parents were immigrants. They worked horribly long hours, and then were expected to take on particularly punishing Hunter shifts"—she shot me an apologetic look—"since they were new to the community, and I guessed the Council wanted them to prove themselves. I suppose their reasoning could have been more sinister, I'm not sure. The Council certainly didn't want me to return to South Africa. I don't know if my family back there fought for me or not, but even if they did, the Hunters Council has money and resources that no individual can match." She shrugged uncomfortably again.

"I dislike that you had an unhappy childhood," I said, frustrated at how powerless the knowledge made me feel. I wanted to go back in time somehow and change things. Give Verity a childhood full of joy and color and an absurd number of pink blankets like she deserved.

"It wasn't too bad, honestly. Or perhaps, I just don't know any different. In some ways, I'm sort of grateful for it? When the Hunters kicked me out, and I lost my entire support network and everyone I cared about, part of the reason I was able to get through it with my delightful charm and sense of humor intact was because I knew I'd already survived something much worse, and I'd come out the other side of that okay. I wasn't going to let them have the satisfaction of breaking me." Verity smiled, all teeth and cunning. "I will live my absolute best life out of spite."

"Good. You did well not to let them break you. Only let your enemies see the weaknesses you want them to see."

Verity laughed. "Surely, I shouldn't let them see *any* weakness?"

"The greatest lesson my mother ever taught me is that there is unlimited potential in perception. To be underestimated is to have a powerful, invisible weapon at your disposal."

Verity was quiet as I worked, staring contemplatively at nothing. Undoubtedly, she thought I was mad, just like everyone else in the realm did. And I was, a little.

There was power in that perception, too.

"Here," I said gruffly once the metal had cooled, holding up the long chain between my claws. Hanging at the bottom of the chain was a circular filigree cage that had once housed an expensive jewel of my mother's. Verity moved closer and I showed her how the cage clicked open around the middle, gesturing for her to set the orb inside it. Her clawless, agile fingers were much better suited to such a delicate task.

Perhaps I could demand she assist in my workshop from time to time? She was my captive after all.

Though, as she closed the necklace with an awestruck look on her face and held still while I lowered it over her head, she didn't *feel* like my captive. If anything, I felt like the one who was ensnared. It wasn't as constricting as I expected the sensation to be.

"It's so beautiful," Verity whispered, plucking the pendant from where it sat between her breasts—a particularly lovely spot, if I said so myself—and holding it up to admire. "You're full of surprises, Your Grace."

She looked up at me, and the moment felt oddly charged, thick with a tension I didn't understand. Verity's gaze dropped to my mouth as she took half a step closer, her front brushing mine.

She paused for a moment, as though waiting for something, though I couldn't determine what. Did she want me to tell her to run? To release my *tentacles*, as she'd so aptly called them?

Or was it something else?

"Do you wish to feed me?" I rasped.

Verity blinked up at me, a slight frown marring her expression. Damn it. I'd gotten it wrong.

"Um, sure. We can do that."

"No, tell me what it is you wanted to do."

Verity laughed awkwardly, taking a step back. "It was nothing. Should we go upstairs then?"

The ground seemed to be crumbling beneath my feet. Things had been going so well, and I'd ruined it with one clumsy misstep. Even her scent was changing, souring into something less settled.

"I did not intend to ruin your mood," I told her solemnly.

Verity's smile softened into something affectionate. Too affectionate for someone like me.

"I know. I'm gonna head upstairs and check on Fester, maybe you can work on one of those fantasies I mentioned later," she added with a wink. She was trying to lighten the mood. Unsure how to assist with that, I simply nodded.

I'd paid close attention to my mate's desires, sensing that this was the one way Verity felt as though I could make her happy here.

And that was fine. She was probably right.

"I'm looking forward to it. I'll leave you to work—thanks again, for the necklace. It's beautiful."

With a slightly shaky smile, Verity left the room, and I felt as though a part of me left with her. The workshop was too quiet, too still.

She'd like the necklace, though. Something had been about to happen after I'd given it to her.

With a renewed sense of confidence, I picked through the pieces of silver for the nicest materials. I'd simply make her another necklace and we would recreate this strange, stolen moment between us. Yes, that was a very wise idea.

I'd try again.

CHAPTER 14

I returned to the library for the remainder of the afternoon, the necklace resting against my chest a constant reminder of the reason I was trying to clean myself into distraction in the first place.

God, that had been awkward. *I* had been awkward. Generally, Theon was the one who lacked social graces, but I'd totally been the bumbling mess in that moment.

We didn't *kiss*. That was not a thing that we did. Why had I gone in for one? Ugh, that was going onto the list of Memories That Would Haunt Me Forever, for sure.

Kissing wasn't a Shade thing in general, from what the mated ex-Hunters had mentioned. Probably because of all the terrifying, flesh-shredding teeth. But it was all a thing that their mates had learned to do safely for them.

But it wasn't a *mate* thing, it was a *love* thing.

Their mates loved them. My mate didn't love me.

For a brief, idiotic moment, I'd expected *affection* when Theon had only ever offered *passion*, and a comfortable life here in his home.

I'd agreed to those terms. Arguably, I'd proposed them, though he was the one who'd decided to make it a forever deal. It wasn't fair on me to move the goalposts now.

Besides, I doubted Theon had it in him to offer more than what he was already giving, even if he wanted to, and I wasn't going to derail the fragile friendship we were forming by demanding it.

I was happy enough. I'd been happy enough in my shitty relationship with Sebastian. I could make myself content anywhere, handle any curveball life threw at me.

Such was the silver lining of carrying around bucketloads of childhood trauma, I guessed.

Setting down the book I'd been dusting aside, I stood up and brushed down my clothes, heading for the corridor.

This grand old manor had been shut away and neglected for far too long, and I needed projects for my own sanity and had nothing but time.

I was pinned to the bed.

That was my first thought when I woke up, the sky still dark outside. I gingerly flexed my legs and shifted my wrists, but they were very much pressed against the mattress, wrapped in something both solid and ephemeral at the same time.

And my cunt was *aching*. That was definitely my second thought. Maybe that had been the first thought, actually. Because I wasn't sure I'd ever been this horny in my life.

"You're awake," Theon rasped in my ear, the warmth of his body covering my back though he was carefully keeping his weight off me.

Huh. Apparently he'd taken my tension-breaking throwaway suggestion seriously.

"You've been playing."

"As you instructed."

"You're a good listener."

Theon huffed what might have been laughter—surely not—but I was distracted by the feel of a probing tentacle between my thighs. My eyes rolled back in my head as it flattened to fit between my body and the sheets, offering just enough stimulation for my already sensitive clit.

"Don't get into the habit of thinking I'll always listen to your instructions, my captive," Theon purred, manipulating the thin strand of shadow into what felt like a forked tongue, massaging my clit at an intensity that had me biting the pillow. "You belong to *me*."

"And you don't belong to me?" I challenged, except I sounded like I was giving it my all in an amateur porno and not even a little bit like the strong, *Independent Women Part 2* baddie I was going for.

Theon hummed.

"How reassuring." That one came out a little sharper. Theon chuckled, shadow tentacles crawling up the backs of my thighs, kneading and pinching my ass.

"I am yours, my captive. Your mate. And you are mine, and one day, you will be my queen. And I am going to keep you very, very happy, and you are going to keep me very well sated, aren't you?"

What were we talking about? Both shadows that had been playing with my ass cheeks were twining around each other, pushing their way into my pussy.

He was different under the cover of darkness. So was I. Perhaps my mistake had been trying to recreate this chemistry in the cold hard light of day.

"You're going to spend most of your days like this, you know," Theon added conversationally. "A drooling, sopping *mess* in the middle of my bed.

Perhaps someday soon with a big round belly, hm? How many children shall I give you? You did say you wanted them."

Oh fuck, oh fuck, oh fuck. Red alert. Sirens were going. I already wanted to come.

"Lots," I breathed, writhing as much as I could with my wrists and ankles still bound.

Theon hummed. "Yes, I think so too. You will make a very good mate for me indeed."

He was saying what he thought I wanted to hear after our awkward moment this afternoon. Smoothing it over the best way he knew how. I didn't read into it, it was a performance and we were both playing our part.

"More," I whined, squirming at the feel of the tentacle breaching me. It was so good and not quite enough all at once. "Wait, Fester—"

"We're in my room," Theon interjected. "It's my bed you've been leaking slick onto for the past half hour."

I had no idea how he'd moved me without me waking up, but I wasn't complaining. Both at the sleep play I'd specifically asked for, and the fact that we weren't actively traumatizing my cat.

"I've been spoiling you," Theon rasped, picking up his pace. "Worshipping this delightful body. I'm a duke. You should really be worshipping me."

My eyes rolled back in my head, the pleasure too intense for me to formulate a snarky reply about how much he enjoyed worshipping me. I was pretty sure this wasn't even doing anything for him—he didn't seem to have that much sensation in his shadow limbs. This was all purely for my benefit.

I gasped as Theon pried my cheeks apart with his thumbs, claws pricking at my skin. I could feel his gaze on me, watching his tentacle sloppily thrusting inside of me, the wet sounds of each movement lewd and obscene. I bucked back against him, desperately trying to meet his movements.

"You are... a revelation," Theon rasped, so quietly that I wasn't sure I was meant to hear it.

"Theon, I need to feel *you*. Fuck me, *please*."

"I was rough with you yesterday."

"I'm not as fragile as you seem to think I am, you know."

Theon's claws traced the outline of a bruise he'd left on my hip in lieu of a response. Spoilsport.

"You don't get my cock today," Theon said firmly, the shadow tentacle moving even faster, expanding in size until it felt like the girth of his knot.

I made a sound I was confident I'd never made before as my pussy clenched and pulsed around him, landing in my own wet spot on the bed as Theon flipped me onto my back. Through bleary eyes, I watched as he scooped slick off the bed and smeared it roughly over his cock, fisting his shaft roughly as he loomed above me.

I could have come from the visual alone. I was banking that image for the Rub Hub later, that was for sure.

In just a few pumps, Theon's cum was spraying over my breasts and stomach, one pulsating tentacle still wringing pleasure out of my borderline oversensitive pussy.

I was splayed out and filthy under his continued perusal, but he didn't look that much more put together.

Theon withdrew his shadows and I laughed breathily, squirming at the odd sensation. "That was excellent, thank you."

"It was," Theon agreed, his voice slightly strangled.

What now?

Should I leave?

Probably.

My legs felt like jelly, but I gingerly edged my way off the bed, cum running down my front as I stood up, despite my best attempt to catch it with my arms.

"Maybe I should clean up in your bathroom?" I suggested, quietly shaking with laughter at the general state of disaster I was in.

"Of course." Theon jumped into action, scooping me off the floor and carrying me to his enormous, grand bathroom, ducking down to turn the taps on without releasing me.

"I don't need a full bath," I pointed out, though I didn't struggle to get out of his hold as Theon carried me into the still-filling tub, setting me on his lap as he sat on the bench that ran around the entire thing.

"You'll sleep more comfortably if you do," he muttered. There was only a faint amount of orb light in here too, and combined with the steam rising off the water, I could only barely make out the planes and angles of his face. Not that his expressions helped particularly—Theon didn't let anyone see anything he didn't want them to see.

"Was that... Did you enjoy that?" Theon asked after a long moment of quiet.

"I did. Did you? It's okay if you didn't, you can tell me."

Of all the things I'd requested, somnophilia had probably been the most out-there, and I'd been pretty sure Theon wouldn't be interested.

His arms tightened around me. "I like having control of your pleasure. I like that you're at my mercy, that you come when I want you to come. That you take what I give you. They're... not urges I've experienced before."

Was smug the wrong reaction in this situation? I liked that I made Theon feel different. We were mates, after all. I wanted to stand out.

"Then again, I don't have *that* much experience."

"With sex?" I asked dubiously. Okay, he was a bit of an introverted mad scientist, but Theon was also hot as fuck. And lived in a decommissioned palace. Surely, he had a long line of willing lovers?

"I didn't have much interest until you."

Fuck.

I leaned into him, pressing my nose to Theon's throat and attempting to gather up the scattered pieces of my composure. I was pretty great at maintaining a healthy—or possibly unhealthy—separation between sex and feelings. I'd gone into this with my eyes open, more open than Theon's even, since he hadn't bothered learning the ramifications of mating before biting me.

But he kept *saying* things and *doing* things, and it was messing with the neat demarcation in my mind. Worse still, as I snuggled into him, a purr rumbled to life in his chest, wrapping around me like a cozy blanket.

How was I meant to not get attached to a guy whose sex drive was in advanced mode just for me? Who made me jewelry, and explored my more obscure kinks, and said he'd give me loads of babies?

It was like Theon had been plucked directly out of my dreams. And he was *mine*, all the way mine. Marked and claimed. Signed, sealed, delivered.

Would it be the worst thing if I allowed myself a smidgen of emotion for him?

Theon grabbed a washcloth from the edge of the tub, dragging it through the water before bringing the material to my chest, cleaning up the mess he'd made of me.

I closed my eyes and let him work, giving myself just tonight, just this moment of peace in the darkness, to appreciate him. To savor him. To be quietly grateful that he'd stormed into that party and demanded an ex-Hunter of his own, and that I'd been filled with enough ennui to volunteer. To be grateful that he had no concept of social mores and had sunk his teeth into me on that very first night, because he'd *wanted* me.

Maybe the rose-tinted glasses would come off eventually, maybe they wouldn't, but for now, I would let myself have this moment with no guilt or self-loathing.

Somewhere along the line, I'd come to really like my mate.

CHAPTER 15

I woke up in my own bed, back in the pajamas Theon must have stripped off me, no mate in sight, but with Fester wrapped around my outstretched arm like a koala, snuffling in his sleep.

If my skin didn't smell like Theon's heady scented soap, I'd have thought I imagined the whole night. I still wasn't entirely sure I hadn't.

Unfortunately, cracking the door open on those squishy feelings had probably been a mistake, because it wasn't quite as easy to close as I'd hoped it would be. My dreams had been haunted by shadow tentacles and mind-melting orgasms, followed by cuddles and long soaks in the tub. My heart had fared a lot better when the porno reel in my brain cut before the aftercare scene started.

"Hey," I grumbled, wiggling my arm to wake Fester up. "The least you could do is wake me up early so my dreams don't start spiraling out of control. Since when do you sleep in?"

He turned his head to the side, immediately falling back to sleep.

Fucker.

Eventually, I managed to shake him off, climbing out of bed to fill his food bowl and get ready for another day of *Extreme Home Makeover: Library Edition*. Damen hadn't been by yesterday, so I opted for a pink fleece sweater with a wide neck that could zip all the way up to my chin to hide the bitemark, pairing it with matching leggings and white sneakers.

Confident that my sweater would do the heavy lifting, I piled my curls on top of my head in a high bun so it would be out of my way while I worked, and grabbed the necklace Theon had given me at the last minute, tucking it beneath my shirt so it lay next to my skin.

Not that I wanted to carry a piece of him around with me all day or anything. That would be dumb and embarrassingly sentimental.

I didn't have any other reason for wearing it, but that was beside the point.

As always, I made for the small sitting room where Aderith always magically appeared with my breakfast. The porch was covered, and the wind was blowing the rain away from the house, so I let myself outside, closing the door behind me so Fester couldn't escape, and taking a seat on the deck.

I thought the incessant mist of rain would bother me, but for the most part, I'd found it kind of cozy. Perhaps because the manor was so large, I wasn't at risk of cabin fever any time soon.

Aderith appeared with my morning tea—I loved meat, but I couldn't stomach it first thing in the morning—and I counted my blessings as I sat under the dry porch, sipping my tea and watching the world go by.

I wasn't worried about how I was going to pay my rent, or where my next meal was going to come from. Fester was happy. I was happy. Theon was... happy? Wasn't he? He was definitely fed, and that was an improvement from when I'd first met him. Overall, this weird situation we'd found ourselves in seemed to be working out pretty well across the board.

I straightened in my seat as Damen appeared from the vegetation-covered path that led to the entry room, immediately spotting me and giving a little wave.

"I'll come up!" he called, heading for the front door. I leaned back in my seat, zipping up my sweater and sipping my tea, confident that Theon would storm up here first and take the one remaining seat just to be an asshole.

Hiding the bitemark wasn't a sustainable solution, but the longer I was here, the less of a big deal the news would be. Maybe we could manage it for a couple more weeks and then I'd make the announcement? I doubted Theon would mind if I told everyone, he appeared only to be going along with it out of respect for my wishes.

Aside from the fact that he'd been a little too bite-happy in the first place without discussing it with me first, Theon had actually been incredibly accommodating of my wishes.

Before I could begin to process that, Theon and Damen came out onto the deck together—one looking significantly happier to be here than the other. I set my teacup down on the table, standing to greet our guest.

"How are you, Verity?" Damen asked with a beaming smile that was all teeth. "Always a pleasure to see you."

"We see far too much of you," Theon grumbled, slipping past me and taking my seat, grabbing my hips to pull me down onto his lap.

Don't get horny, don't get horny, don't get horny.

Poor, single Damen spent most of his time with Allerick or Soren, both of whom were mated off. He was probably really sick of horny ex-Hunter pheromones.

"You know this is how it has to be," Damen replied lightly, not missing a thing as he took the seat angled toward us, watching as Theon passed me my cup and discreetly adjusted my sweater, keeping my neck completely concealed.

Did that look suspicious?

Maybe.

No, probably not. We were fine. Shit. Maybe I should just say something now.

Aderith appeared with more tea and a plate of small gray sweet cakes, and if Shades could blush, I swear she would have at the charming smile Damen sent her.

"How's the tour going?" Theon asked him, showing a frankly astounding level of civility.

Damen made a discontented sound. "Meridia's rebellion didn't entirely die with her. It's been... a little stressful from a security perspective."

Huh.

I'd never thought of Theon as a serious threat to Allerick's reign, but if Damen was telling him this... did that mean *he* didn't think Theon's threats had any heat either? Theon was nodding along like he understood completely and this was entirely reasonable conversation for the two of them to be having.

I didn't get it at all. Maybe it was just my only-childness showing.

"I executed a particularly eager follower of hers just the other day," Theon replied, entirely relaxed.

"Excuse me?" I spluttered, coughing up half my tea. "You did *what?* When?"

"Executed. The other day," Theon repeated slowly, as if my comprehension was the problem here.

"When were you going to mention that?!"

He shrugged. "Never, probably. Should I have?"

Damen laughed. "That does seem like something the lady of the house might want to know. You really shouldn't be going around doing vigilante executions, though. The Council of Shades will get mad."

Theon snorted. "They offered to be my own personal army. I think the Councilors would find that more offensive."

"That's why you killed them?" Damen asked, sounding more curious than anything else.

"I killed them for watching Verity."

Damen nodded. "That seems reasonable."

"Does it?" I asked, though I was oddly flattered in a way that probably required a psychiatric evaluation.

"Yes," Theon replied easily, squeezing my middle lightly.

"Are you on track to have the court here tomorrow?" Damen asked, apparently satisfied with that answer.

"So long as you're not expecting too much," Theon replied off-handedly. "I have no interest in feeding an entire court."

"Good thing you're not a king then," Damen shot back, a teasing smile on his face. I held my breath, not at all confident that Theon was going to respond well to Damen's ribbing.

But he just scoffed. "Allerick is welcome to that particular perk of leadership."

Huh. Was Theon... the Brain?

As in *Pinky and the Brain*?

He talked a big game about taking over the world and how he'd do a better job, but ultimately his plans were pretty toothless.

Did that make me Pinky? I smoothed down my pastel pink sweater. That seemed like kismet, honestly.

"Verity, was there anything you wanted to discuss?" Damen asked before shoving a cake in his mouth.

Theon remained entirely relaxed beneath me. Maybe he was getting used to having Damen around.

"No, I don't think so." Being a real team with Theon meant discussing the reveal of the mating mark with him first, right? It had been a long time since I'd been part of a team with anyone, but I was determined to do it right, especially since he was clearly making an effort too.

"Anything you need from the human realm?"

I grinned at Damen. "I'll make a list."

He laughed. "Well, I'll be back tomorrow with the court, you can give it to Astrid then."

I attempted to stand to say goodbye, but Theon kept me firmly pinned in place on his lap.

Damen laughed, already letting himself out. "I'll see you tomorrow."

We sat in peaceful silence, watching Damen disappear down the path and into the vegetation as the rain continued to fall around us. Once Damen had gone, Theon gently unzipped my sweater, pulling it out of the way so his teeth could scrape over the bite mark.

"We should tell them tomorrow. That we're mated," I said quietly, resting my temple against the curved edge of his horn while I stared out at the forest beyond.

Theon hummed. "Undoubtedly, many will have opinions on it. Are you ready to face those?"

My gut reaction was *fuck no*, but I was pushing past my usual coping mechanism of 'hope the problem goes away on its own.'

"It'll be fine," I replied with more bravado than I felt, setting my empty cup down and twisting so I was sitting sideways across his lap. "You were getting along well with Damen?"

Theon huffed. "I imagine Damen gets along well with most everyone he encounters. Surely, he should have been the first to secure a Hunter bride," he added under his breath, sounding genuinely confused about it.

"I don't think it was for lack of trying. He just hasn't connected with anyone yet."

"We didn't *connect* upon first meeting, and it's turned out fine thus far. He should simply kidnap a Hunter and work it out from there."

I laughed, pressing a kiss to his cheek. "You didn't kidnap me, babycakes."

"I *essentially* kidnapped you."

"Still no."

"Did I not march into the midst of the court and demand my own Hunter? Admit that you are my captive," he demanded softly, gripping the back of my neck so he could stroke the bite mark again.

I tilted my head back, giving him better access. "No. Admit that I came willingly. Because we *connected*."

He scoffed. "Liar."

"Okay, we didn't connect right that second, but I knew there was something there."

"You're still lying."

"I *hoped* there was something there," I laughed, nudging him with my shoulder. "And I was right. Right?"

It was an excruciatingly vulnerable question, and I silently braced myself for the worst. For Theon to tell me that no, actually. That this relationship was purely transactional, and I'd read something into it that wasn't there.

It would only be my own stupid fault for expecting any more from Mr. You-Are-My-Prisoner, even with the moments of sweetness he'd shown.

"I am more attached to you than I expected to be."

That was the Theon equivalent of 'I'd die for you, my love,' and I refused to believe otherwise.

I twisted in his lap so I was facing him, draping my arms over his shoulders. "Good answer. I'd like to kiss you now."

I'd already panicked and backed off once before because his body language hadn't been encouraging enough for me to close the distance, but I wasn't going to chicken out this time. I was going to use my words like a motherfucking *adult*. Mentally, I gave myself a little pat on the back for my maturity.

Theon frowned slightly, leaning forward to press his lips to my forehead.

Huh, maybe that was why he'd been giving me mixed signals. In so many ways, Theon seemed to know everything about the developments between Hunters and Shades—from a spy of his at court, I presumed—but maybe he hadn't heard about *this*.

I shifted my hands, gently cupping his sharp jaw. "Like this... may I?"

"Of course." There was a small flutter of delight in my stomach at the way he was just... letting me do whatever I wanted. I had no intention of abusing his trust, of course, but I was amazed he'd so easily given it to me.

As I leaned in, brushing my lips gently against his at first, I felt like a shy teenager experiencing my first kiss all over again. There was an element of newness to it—Theon's lips were much firmer than any human's, and almost leathery in texture, so I had to move mine a little differently—but it was also just *him*. Even when he was hunting me down, pinning me to the floor and wrecking my insides, he still made me feel like a girl with my first crush.

I teased at the seam of his mouth with my tongue, and while *I* couldn't smell myself perfuming the air with arousal, I was absolutely confident that I was when his tongue brushed tentatively against mine.

"You're a fast learner," I said in a muffled voice, because he was also an enthusiastic learner and wasn't ready to let go of me yet.

Theon let out a rumbling growl of agreement, his arms banding more tightly around me, one hand gripping my hair, tugging my head back and encouraging me to open for him. Within seconds, he'd gone from light and unsure to tonguefucking my throat, and I was cursing myself for not straddling him before I'd started this game, because I could desperately use some friction right now.

The door opened with a bang, and we sprung apart so fast that Theon's fang scraped my lip, the faintest trace of coppery blood hitting my tongue. Only Theon's fast reflexes saved me from falling off his lap completely.

"Your Grace," Wilder panted, skidding to a stop in front of us, looking panicked. "She's gone. Melody-Rainywillow is gone."

"Gone?" Theon rasped, pulling me further into him as if he could shield me. "Gone where?"

Wilder swallowed nervously. "The human realm. She and your mother fought about Melody-Rainywillow's plan, and then she left."

Theon's shadows bristled with agitation. He didn't explode with anger the way I'd expected him to, though. Just sighed heavily before climbing to his feet, taking me with him and placing me gently on my feet, though he didn't let me go.

"Stubborn, boneheaded *child*," Theon muttered. "She's going to get herself killed. How long ago?"

"A few hours."

Theon's shadows cracked around us like whips without connecting with anything, and I winced. "Why am I only hearing about it now?"

"Your mother tried to follow. Tried to bring her back without... inconveniencing you."

"Without *telling* me," Theon corrected. Wilder nodded in agreement, looking just as disapproving. "My mother is no warrior. What did she think she was going to achieve? Ludicrous. I will go and fetch Rainy."

"Hold on," I interjected, twisting out of his hold so I could face him, while holding onto his forearm. "Theon, we need to alert the palace first."

"Absolutely not."

"You're not allowed in the human realm—"

Theon straightened. "I don't take orders from my little brother."

"That little brother is the *king*, and responsible for the safety of every Shade in the realm—"

"He is not responsible for me," Theon growled. "His edict is ridiculous. I know exactly where Rainy is—we have discussed the spot for years—you and I will simply go there now and fetch her. I will deal with her as I see fit once we are back home."

He grabbed my hand, tugging me into the sitting room and heading for the corridor. He'd moved so quickly that he hadn't been as mindful of his claws as he usually was, and I sucked in a breath as he broke the skin on my thumb.

"*We?*" I asked, stumbling on behind him.

"Of course. Did you not hear what I said earlier? The remnants of Meridia's followers have been seeking me out. They've been watching *you*. I cannot abide by that. You aren't safe here."

"I'm pretty sure I'm safer here than in the human realm, Theon." We were already heading down the stairs, one of his shadow limbs wrapped around my waist, holding on to me. "Wait, I think we should discuss this—"

"There's nothing to discuss. You are not safe anywhere I am not, Verity. You are *mine* to protect." He paused for a moment, evidently scenting my blood in the air and holding up my thumb for his concerned inspection.

"It's fine, it'll heal on its own," I assured him, pulling my hand away. "You could leave me at the palace if you didn't want me to stay here without you—"

"At the palace? Where Damen could steal you away at any moment?" Theon snorted. "Absolutely not."

"*Damen?*" I repeated incredulously, contemplating socking Theon in the shadow limb on principle. "Are you serious, right now? Theon, I'm not interested in Damen, and Damen is not interested in me. You're not thinking clearly."

"You're wrong. He wants you for himself—"

"He does *not*—"

"I'm not leaving you here," Theon snapped, all but dragging me out the front door toward the entry room. Wilder kept pace with him, watching me nervously. At least someone else realized this was an idiotic idea.

"Wilder, go and fetch my mother. Bring her here to wait for our return. I don't want her taking any more ill-advised trips into the human realm, thinking she's being helpful."

"Yes, Your Grace," Wilder agreed, following us into the entry room and pulling the door shut behind us. We were immediately encased in darkness, and I felt, rather than saw, Wilder leave.

"Don't do this," I told Theon quietly.

The shadow limb around my waist flexed in response to my words. "You are *my* mate. I trust no one else with your safety."

"Trust *me* with my safety. Trust that *I* want you, and only you. Theon, don't let jealousy cloud your judgment—you know this isn't a good idea."

He'd done so well at respecting my wishes so far, even when I hadn't realized he was doing it. But he wouldn't be deterred.

Theon's jealousy when it came to his brothers was so much worse than I realized, and now it was too late to do anything about it.

His mind was made up.

CHAPTER 16

My panic had made me irrational. I could see that now.

The canyon where I always exited into the human realm—a deserted spot by night that I'd never seen a Hunter in—was already far lighter than I anticipated it would be. Not so light that I couldn't enter it, but the sun was rising, and fast.

If Rainy wasn't close by, then I would have no choice but to turn around and go back.

My grip on Verity had vanished the moment we had stepped into the human realm and I had shifted into my ephemeral form, and I hated that I couldn't hold on to her. While I couldn't *feel* the strength of the wind, I could hear how loud it was.

"Theon," Verity said nervously, drawing my attention. My olfactory system worked the same way in this realm, and Verity's scent was loudly broadcasting her misery. "This isn't a good idea."

Her teeth were chattering with cold, arms wrapped tightly around her midsection. She'd only followed me a few steps out from beneath the dark, rocky overhang where I liked to enter to the human realm.

Fuck. I was screwing this all up. I couldn't possibly move at my fastest speed in order to find Rainy with Verity here. I couldn't even leave her here in this secluded spot, not when the elements were causing her harm.

"*You're right*," I said, hoping she could hear me the way my fellow Shades could when we were in this form. Verity's eyes widened in surprise, so I guessed she had. "*I... I was hasty. I'll return to you to the shadow realm. Wilder should be back with my mother, you can stay with them—*"

Before I could finish speaking, a particularly large gust of wind blew through the tunnel that the rock formations created, buffeting Verity's slight figure.

That was all it took.

She was so *fragile*.

One hard gust of wind and she lost her footing, the steep, uneven ground working against her. I grabbed for her, my hands slipping right through her torso as she fell slowly backward, fighting with every muscle in her body to stay upright.

But it was too late.

With a petrified scream that would haunt me for the rest of my days, Verity fell down the rocky embankment, landing hard on her back, her head bouncing slightly as it hit the ground.

"*Verity!*" I shouted, hovering above her, having followed her the full way down. "*Verity! Open your eyes immediately!*"

She didn't open her eyes. Her chest rose and fell, and a small trickle of blood seeped from somewhere beneath her hairline, soaking into the rocky earth.

"*Verity, my love,*" I said, lowering my trembling voice, aiming for a more soothing tone. "*I made a mistake. I shouldn't have brought you here, you were right. I'll take you home now, and you can rest. I will care for you. Just open your eyes, my love. I need you to walk a few steps for me. I will guide you back into the in-between and carry you the rest of the way. Just stand for me. Open your eyes, my love, and stand for me.*"

Silence. Except for the sound of that treacherous wind blowing, there was nothing. Verity's eyes didn't open. Her limbs remained splayed at awkward angles in the dirt. The sun persisted in rising.

"I'll take you home and care for you, and you will be well. I'll never ask anything of you again. Please, Verity, wake up for me."

The fear was paralyzing. I'd never struggled with indecision before, but this situation felt so helpless. There was no good outcome. Not even the possibility of one.

"I will return for you, my love. I'm getting help. I am getting help. Just… just don't die. I will be very cross with you if you die. You will come home with me, and I will love you as you should be loved. Do not die."

I floated up the embankment and into the cool darkness of the cavern, immediately passing through it and reaching for the darkness of the in-between. As soon as my form solidified, I was running faster than I'd ever run, *feeling* my hands covered in Verity's blood, even though my incorporeal limbs had passed straight through her the moment I'd reached for her.

She'd fallen so far.

I'd told Rainy about that spot, out in the desert, surrounded by beautiful rock formations. It was a safe place to appear under the cover of darkness. Not as convenient as materializing in a city, but with almost no chance of encountering a Hunter.

For very good reason. It wasn't a safe location for a human. If I'd have been in *this* form, subject to the will of gravity, I would have never considered it a convenient location for anything.

How could I have been so stupid? Verity was so fragile, and I'd hurt her because of my own sick jealousy. My obsessive need to keep her to myself. What if she never woke up?

No, I refused to accept that.

I pushed myself faster and harder than I'd ever moved in my life, all but throwing myself out of the portal in front of the palace, and coming to a stumbling stop in front of half of Allerick's court and the king himself, decked out in all of their finery, presumably returning from a stop on their tour.

"What are you doing here?" Damen asked, surprised. "Where's Verity?"

"I need help," I rasped, looking at the king. "She's hurt. Please. Help me bring her home."

Allerick straightened instantly. "Where?"

"The human realm."

Mutters broke out amongst the courtiers, but I didn't care about that. Whatever the cost, whatever Allerick demanded of me, I would give it gladly. Anything to get Verity back.

"She can't walk," I added. "She's not conscious."

"Astrid—" Allerick began.

"Already on it," the queen's sister announced, jogging up to the entry room with Captain Soren in tow. "Show us."

I didn't hesitate, guiding us straight back into the in-between. Astrid jumped on Soren's back, allowing us to move faster as we sprinted back to the exit point I'd used, but now it was burning, warning us away.

"Fuck," Astrid muttered, jumping off Soren's back. "Find somewhere nearby. You'll both have to stay here—"

"Absolutely not," Soren cut in, already in motion as we searched for a suitable entry point.

"Absolutely, *yes*. You can't go out there in daylight, I can. Theon, you're going to need to tell me what I'm walking into. What happened?"

"She fell," I rasped. "The wind... And then she lost her footing. We were high on the rocks—"

"Did you walk her off a fucking cliff or something?! What the hell is wrong with you?" Astrid yelled. "Soren, get me through there right fucking now."

He found a dark enough point of entry, gliding through it before reappearing a moment later, shaking his head. "It's a narrow crevice in the rocks, too narrow for any human body to fit through. Astrid, you're no use to anyone if you're injured yourself," he added, cutting off her objections.

Astrid swore, pacing back and forth.

"How populated is the area?" Soren demanded. "What are the chances of someone coming across and taking her to a human healer?"

"I believe it's well-traveled during daylight hours," I replied, hating the idea of Verity being taken away by human authorities. She'd be so frightened when she woke up.

"Shit, I need to get out of here. If she's moved to a hospital, we might *never* find her," Astrid pointed out.

I cleared my throat. "We'll be able to find her."

Soren and Astrid turned to face me at the same time, horror and suspicion written all over both of them.

"You didn't," Astrid said flatly. "Tell me you didn't."

"I did. Verity is my mate."

CHAPTER 17

M a'am, can you hear me?"

There were voices all around me, people jostling my aching body, forcing me to move.

"Everything is going to be okay," a woman said in a voice that was somehow both calming and efficient. Like she did this all the time. I sternly told my eyelids to get out of the way so I could see her, let her know that I was… well, not great, but I'd be okay. But my eyelids weren't in the mood to cooperate. They felt as though they weighed a thousand pounds each, but it was probably the least of my problems, in all honesty, because at least they didn't hurt. Everything else *hurt*.

Was I dying? If so, this was not a comfortable transition to the afterlife and didn't bode well for me.

There were conversations happening above me, though my focus slipped in and out, despite my best efforts. Someone mentioned the hospital. Okay.

Okay. Not dead.

Yet.

Unless they took dead people to the hospital?

Maybe.

It didn't matter. I didn't want to stay here, regardless. I wanted to go *home*, and home wasn't here. I had to leave.

After a little nap. Yes, that was a good idea. I'd just take a little nap, and then I'd explain to the nice doctors that I didn't belong in this world, and be on my merry way.

An irritating, incessant beeping woke me up. Before I'd even opened my eyes, the sterile scent of industrial cleaning solution and fluorescent lights above me gave my location away.

How had I ended up here?

Right. There was an accident. Theon had been there. We'd been perched precariously in a rocky canyon. It was windy.

I swallowed—more out of reflex than need. My throat was parched, and tight with the need to cry, though I was probably too dehydrated for tears. I couldn't remember *exactly* what happened to leave me like this, but I knew I'd been feeling unsafe. Wobbly. And the wind had been *so* scary...

I blinked my scratchy eyes open slowly, taking in the unfamiliar hospital room, complete with bright overhead lights that made my already aching head throb more.

This was not a Shade-friendly spot. There was no way Theon could materialize into the bright environment and squirrel me away back to the shadow realm.

That realization spiraled into a slew of other terrifying ones. People were going to have questions for me. Was I considered a missing person? Had anyone filed a report?

And if they had, what was I meant to say?

I forced myself to take a few deep, steadying breaths before I devolved into a full-blown panic attack, the stupid heart monitor filling the room with my stressed-out pulse.

I could just lie, right? Lying was still a solid option.

I heard someone coming into the room, and while I contemplated just slamming my eyes shut and pretending to still be asleep, my heart rate was probably giving me away.

A young man in dark blue scrubs entered the room, dark red hair pushed haphazardly back from his face. *Lucas*, I read, spotting his name tag. His eyes lingering on mine long enough to know I was awake, and yet he didn't acknowledge me at all. Instead, he moved around the bed, checking and noting various things, tutting at something and humming in approval at something else.

I hadn't spent enough time in hospitals to know if this was normal or not.

It didn't feel normal.

He stopped at the end of the bed, attention finally returning to my face, his gaze impassive. "You're a long way from home, Verity de Jager."

My breath caught in my throat. Was he a Hunter? They could be found in all professions and were especially drawn to shift work because of their sleep cycles.

Fuck, fuck, fuck. Just trying to formulate some kind of coherent response made my head throb. I did my best to look confused, which didn't require much effort.

"You're still in Utah, in case you were wondering. You took quite the tumble. Fortunately, you were found by some early morning hikers not too far from Jacob Hamblin Arch before the situation got any worse."

My head hurt. My bones hurt. My entire body hurt.

"Hunters across the world have been told to look out for you, you know. You and the others who ran away. Or were you stolen? There's some debate over how consensual your defection to the shadow realm was. I'd certainly love to know how you ended up at Coyote Gulch."

He grabbed the cup of water on the table next to the bed, holding the straw to my lips, and I was too thirsty to be prideful about it. With as much self-control as I could manage, I slowly sipped at the water, wondering if it had ever tasted as good as it did at that moment.

"I didn't want to tell them you were here," Lucas said, observing me having an emotional moment over water like I was a science experiment. "I had to. We all have our part to play, but I just want a quiet life. Bringing half of the high-ranking Hunters in the country down on me wouldn't have been my first choice. You've put me in an awkward position."

My brain felt like sludge, but through the thick haze of... drugs?— probably drugs—I remembered Theon's words.

"To be underestimated is to have a powerful, invisible weapon at your disposal."

It was the *only* weapon I had at my disposal, and I wasn't going to waste it.

"I think there's been some kind of mistake," I rasped, glancing around the room with wide eyes. "You have me confused with someone else."

Lucas frowned. "You're Verity de Jager. From Colorado."

"Yes," I agreed, blinking sluggishly at him and trying to decide how much to say. My entire knowledge of amnesia came from daytime soap operas, and I wasn't sure if I was overselling or underselling it. Should I act more confused? When was he going to ask me who the president was?

Lucas cocked his head to the side. "I'm going to get the doctor. She's human, don't mention anything about what we just discussed."

I made a point of looking extra confused at that. Or I tried to, at least. I wasn't entirely sure my facial muscles were cooperating with me, everything hurt too much to pinpoint specifics.

Lucas's suspicious expression stayed fixed in place as he headed for the door, and I did my best to hide my trembling hands beneath the sheet.

I wasn't smart enough for this. I was Verity de Jager, pet store sales associate in the human realm, and aimless drifter in the shadow realm.

But that wasn't going to cut it, because I was also Verity de Jager, Duchess of Lindow. My mate was a force of nature, and he made things happen. And while sometimes he made stupid things happen, I still admired his drive. And we were a team, I wasn't about to let the side down now.

No, I had to be smart. I had to take whatever advantages I could get to keep myself safe until I figured out an escape plan.

"Where's my boyfriend?" I asked before Lucas could leave the room, making sure I sounded as weak and pitiful as possible. "Where's Sebastian?"

CHAPTER 18

Once darkness had fallen, I followed the pull of the mate bond into the human realm, landing in a dark, dingy alleyway with Soren and Astrid directly behind me. Unfortunately, Soren and I could go no farther. The alleyway was dark, but light spilled into the mouth of it from a brightly lit street, limiting our range.

"*That way,*" I said, pointing my incorporeal hand in the direction the bond was telling me to go.

Astrid darted off without further instruction, and Soren swore as he floated after her, stopping right at the edge of the pool of light.

Rainy had returned of her own volition several hours earlier, and was now cooped up at Allerick's palace with Mother. I was grateful that my sister was safe, but I'd been too furious to even contemplate seeing her. Until Verity was safely back at home where she belonged, I wouldn't be able to focus on anything else.

"*You've really made a mess of things, Theon,*" Soren said darkly, his cloaked head turning to face me. "*You know you cannot go free after this. The ex-Hunters in the shadow realm are under the protection of the Crown. You* lost *her. Damaged her. There will be consequences.*"

"Verity is not a possession," I snapped, shame curdling in my gut at the way I'd considered her as such once upon a time.

"No, she's not," Soren conceded. *"But she is vulnerable in our realm, and the protections extended to her are overreaching accordingly. To say nothing of your mating. If Verity were here and I asked her if you had her whole and full-hearted consent to claim her as your mate, what answer would I receive, Theon?"*

I had no response for that, which was a response in itself. The answer was no. I'd wanted Verity, so I'd taken her. At the time, her lack of outrage had seemed like a positive sign—as though she hadn't *really* minded my high-handedness. In hindsight, having come to know Verity, I understood that she hadn't experienced a life filled with joy, unlike her bright demeanor suggested.

Verity hadn't been outraged because she hadn't expected any better for herself. She hadn't considered her own happiness at all.

A few moments later, Astrid reappeared, her expression grim. "It's a hospital, so at least Verity is receiving medical attention. Unfortunately, one of the guys vaping across the street is a Hunter from Seattle, and we are definitely *not* in Seattle."

"What does that mean?" Soren asked.

"It means that someone recognized her and called in the hometown troops." Astrid's expression was stricken. "They're going to be all over that building, she's too valuable to them to risk getting away."

"Then what can we do?" The desperation of the situation was bearing down heavily on me now. I'd foolishly thought that so long as the mating bond led me to her, Astrid would find a way to handle the task of physically getting Verity back to the in-between, and I could simply carry her from there.

But this...

"We can monitor from afar," Astrid replied grimly. "I can make inquiries with sympathetic contacts here, but the Hunters are going to be hypervigilant. I'm not sure there's anything we can do until Verity is able to get away from them on her own steam."

"I refuse to accept that's true."

"It doesn't matter what you think, regardless," Soren cut in evenly. *"Until your fate has been decided, you're going to the Pit."*

There was no way to mark the passage of time in the Pit. The blinding orb light never dimmed, not even for the prisoners to sleep, so as not to compromise the security. Meal delivery seemed to be sporadic. Infrequently, these meals were served with a small orb of power on the tray to keep us fed enough to survive, though I had returned them all intact.

The room I'd been assigned was nicer than the cells most criminals were given, but it was still very much a jail.

And for once, I couldn't resent Allerick, nor his decision to put me here. I'd been entrusted with the greatest treasure in the shadow realm, and I hadn't taken care of her. Verity was stuck there because of me. The strained, muffled bond in my chest a constant reminder that we were on opposite sides of the in-between.

Soren had informed me that they had eyes on Verity's location, and if she was moved, then I would be brought back under supervision to follow her through the bond again. Thus far, she appeared to still be in the healing facility.

It was a disconcerting thought. How long did humans usually stay in such a place?

The helplessness was crushing. If time were mine to control, I would take us back to that kiss under the porch while the rain fell peacefully around us, and do everything differently. I would have listened to Verity's suggestion to go to the palace for help retrieving Rainy. If I'd gone to the human realm as part of that delegation, I would have insisted Verity stay safely with her friends at Elverston House.

She'd have still been there on my return. Perhaps, she would have even been happy to see me? It seemed for a moment as though something was growing between us. Something that brought her joy.

"Theon." I turned sharply at my sister's quiet voice, finding her standing at the bars of my cell, more contrite than I'd ever seen her.

Anger rose, but ebbed away again just as quickly. I was too tired to hold on to it.

It wasn't Rainy's fault that Verity got hurt. It was mine.

"Theon," Rainy sniffled. "I'm sorry. I didn't mean for all of this to happen."

"I know," I replied, staring up at the stone ceiling.

"I shouldn't have gone. I should have listened to you."

Were the circumstances not so dire, the admission that she was wrong would have been amusing.

"Please don't be mad at me. I didn't mean for Verity to get hurt."

"And I don't blame you for that." Verity hadn't *wanted* to go to the human realm. I'd dragged her back there because of my own stupid jealousy. That error had been mine, and mine alone.

"I can help you get her back, though," Rainy said earnestly. "I was right. I'm *so* fast in the human realm—"

"Enough," I said firmly. "I know what it is to be young and want to prove yourself, Rainy. I know it better than most. But you are not invincible. Sometimes, the best course of action is to listen to those who know better, even if we don't like what they have to say. To at least *consider* our options before we take them. Return to the palace. Stay there with Mother. Do not do anything rash. Am I understood?"

I wasn't even sure how she'd gotten here in the first place. Mother clearly wasn't doing a good job at keeping an eye on her wayward daughter.

"I could break you out—"

"Don't even finish that sentence," I clipped. Rainy was a resourceful child; I had full confidence that if anyone could break me out of the Pit, it was her. But I wasn't going to run from the consequences of my actions. I would face up to them, no matter how dire. For Verity's sake.

"What are you doing here?" Damen asked from farther down the corridor, making Rainy jump. "You should really have been escorted by a guard or something."

"I was just leaving," Rainy said hastily, shooting me a last lingering look before scampering off, leaving Damen and Allerick standing in her place in front of the guards.

"Any news?" I asked, not stirring from the bed. This was a new development. Usually, Damen came alone to provide updates.

"No," Damen answered. "Astrid paid a contact to try get into the hospital as Verity's friend to visit, but she is well guarded by Hunters. There was no way for them to get past."

I nodded silently, suspecting as much.

"You need to feed," Allerick said quietly, observing me from the other side of the bars. I thought once that this was where my brothers would enjoy seeing me most, but neither of them appeared to be deriving any joy from it.

"I'm not touching a single drop of power that doesn't come from Verity."

"Your dedication is admirable, but you're no good to Verity if you're dead," Damen pointed out.

"Damen, could you leave us for a moment?" Allerick asked. There was a long pause before I heard Damen's footsteps heading back down the hall. After some fussing with the lock, Allerick let himself into my cell, crossing the room to sit at the end of the bed, next to my legs.

Truly, I mustn't have been any kind of threat for him to come in here.

For a long while, we sat in suffocating silence, and I wondered what Allerick was even doing here. We'd interacted very little over the course of our lives—that dinner party that felt like a different lifetime ago was probably the most we'd ever spoken.

"I fear I haven't been a good brother to you all these years," Allerick eventually said, studiously avoiding looking at me.

I snorted. "We share a father, but we're not brothers."

The resentment I felt at Allerick and Damen's close relationship rose dangerously close to the surface before I ruthlessly suppressed it once more. It was foolish to feel jealousy over that. There were ten years between Allerick and me, and I'd been intentionally raised in isolation, away from my siblings. The only blame that could be assigned was toward our father, who was many years dead now.

"I give myself grace for my actions in my youth," Allerick continued. "But when I came of age, and more pertinently, when I came to the throne, there was no excuse for my actions. I suppose I thought that because you were older than me that you didn't need me."

"I don't need you."

"You did, though," Allerick sighed. "You needed friends. You needed family. The court—the realm—followed my lead. Had I worked harder to reconcile the change of position between us, they would have done the same. You would not have been so neglected."

"I only need Verity," I hissed, desperately trying to staunch the hidden wound his words had opened.

"You certainly need her too," Allerick agreed evenly. "I can see that now. She's your Ophelia."

I didn't have a response for that. I hadn't expected him to be so... understanding. We'd never found common ground before, but he looked like a male who understood what it was to have his life turned inside out by love.

"Why is it that you're here?" I asked, weary down to my bones.

"The Councilors do not believe I can be impartial in your case," Allerick sighed. "They have taken the lead on everything related to it—including ordering a search on your home."

"Okay." I had nothing to hide. There were plenty of documents stating what I *would* do if I were king, but I'd never written down any treasonous intent to take the position for myself.

"They discovered the notes in your study. Your suggestions to better integrate the ex-Hunters who relocate to the shadow realm." Allerick paused for a moment. "They were very good. Far more comprehensive than anything I'd come up with."

I appreciated how the words sounded like they were dragged from the very depths of his being.

"Unfortunately, the Councilors are fixated on one particular part of your suggestions..."

I closed my eyes, a wry smile twisting my lips. "The punishments?"

Allerick made an uncomfortable sound of assent.

How very neat, that I'd drafted my own death warrant. How exceptionally organized of me.

"You should not feel that you need to defend me," I said, opening my eyes to stare up at the ceiling once more. "You must not feel conflicted in any way about this, Allerick. I would vastly prefer you put me from your mind entirely. Finding Verity and bringing her safely home, that is what matters. It is the *only* thing that matters."

"I think you'll find I'm very intelligent and capable of caring about more than one thing at a time," Allerick replied impatiently. "However, I do believe you are at least partially correct. If Verity cares for you as much as Damen claims she does"—*Damen had claimed as such?*—"then she is your best and only defense."

Allerick stood, looking down at me with so much pity in his eyes that I should have felt frustration or shame, but there was no room for that. No room for any emotion beyond despair.

"Have heart, brother. We have no intention of giving up. Verity *will* come home."

But to what home? To mine? Would I be here to greet her upon her return?

Or would the death warrant I'd already signed have taken me from her by then?

CHAPTER 19

Your fiancé is here," Doctor Torres said kindly, giving me a gentle smile. I steadied my breathing, grateful that the doctor couldn't smell the undoubtedly sour pheromones I was putting out with that news. This was the trap I'd sprung for myself in the hopes of avoiding a bigger one, but it still had teeth.

That Sebastian was claiming to be my fiancé had my hackles rising, though. What the hell was he playing at? This was *my* made-up scenario, not his.

Hearing his footsteps outside the door, I quickly wriggled down in the bed, pulling the sheet up to my chin to cover the mating mark, but freeing my hands from under the blanket so I looked slightly less corpse-like.

"Verity," Sebastian said, rushing in and all but collapsing next to my bed, his shaking hands gently gripping my fingers in a convincing show of relief. I flinched instantly, my body reacting before my brain could catch up.

Get your shit together, Verity. He's meant to be your boyfriend-fiancé, even—for god's sake.

"Easy," Doctor Torres murmured to Sebastian, while giving me a strained smile.

"Right." Sebastian shoved his sandy-blond hair out of his face. "I'm just so relieved to see her. Sorry. I know I need to... take it slow."

Apparently, he'd been debriefed on my *condition* already, which I supposed made sense.

What didn't make sense was the way he was acting. I'd expected him to let me down easy—tell me that I was mistaken and we'd been broken up for years. But I'd also expected him to hang around, and inadvertently, set himself up as a buffer between myself and the Council, who'd be foaming at the mouth to pick my brain apart.

It had been ten years, but I suspected that Sebastian was still the same guy at heart. A *nice* guy. A hero. The white knight who rode in to save the damsels from all of their distress. He couldn't help himself.

Maybe I'd rolled the dice wrong on that front, though. Was he playing along as an act of kindness? Or was he playing 4D chess with me?

Had he always been such a convincing actor?

"I'm so glad you remember me, baby," he said, seeming genuinely emotional about the revelation.

Oh, yes. I remembered Sebastian perfectly. I remembered exactly what a spineless little mama's boy he'd been. I remembered how I'd been good enough for him until I wasn't; how he'd thrown me to the wolves the moment things got hard.

I *remembered*.

"Things are a little... fuzzy," I managed, giving him a watery smile. Tentatively, I reached for his hand, my stomach turning at the feeling of his damp, sweaty palm and clawless fingertips beneath mine.

As far as he was concerned, I was behaving perfectly naturally. I'd always been pretty meek and happy to let him lead when we were together. Probably because he'd done such a good job at making me feel like an idiot who was incapable of making decisions for myself.

"I know, baby. It's all going to be okay, I'm here now. What do you remember?"

The doctor made a quiet sound of disapproval as she fussed with my records over in the corner, but the opportunity to try to figure out what he was playing at was too good to pass up.

"We live in Denver..." I said slowly.

"That's right, baby. We live in a ranch-style house we bought two years ago. We just finished the basement so we'd have plenty of room for a big family, remember?"

My uterus curled in on itself.

Oh, he wasn't fucking around. He really wanted me to think we'd been together *this whole time*.

I frowned, squinting a little to make it look like my head hurt. "We started dating in high school. You gave me a corsage with pink carnations for prom. We took a trip to Jackson Lake with some friends for graduation."

Sebastian nodded so encouragingly that I almost second-guessed my own sanity. Maybe I *had* hit my head harder than I thought, and the shadow realm had all been a fever dream. We had talked about doing up a ranch house one day.

But my thumb brushed over the scar on the side of my finger where Theon's claw had broken the skin, centering me. If I could have touched my mating mark without drawing Sebastian's attention, I would have, but I didn't want to risk it.

I am Verity de Jager. Kind-of Duchess of Lindow. I live in the shadow realm with my monster mate, Theon, Duke of Lindow. I have friends there. A home there. An errant sister-in-law there.

I'm going to find my way back.

I'm going to find my way home.

I ran Theon's words through my mind again, holding on to them for comfort. *"To be underestimated is to have a powerful, invisible weapon at your disposal."*

I was out of my depth and no battle strategist, but Theon kind of was. Or he'd at least been trained as one. I trusted his judgment.

"I'm so sorry this happened," Sebastian said, staring intently into my eyes. I'd once found his soulful green gaze *so* dreamy, and now everything about him seemed insincere. It was all a mask to disguise who he really was underneath. "You were so determined to go on this hiking trip, and I should have tried harder to dissuade you. I take complete responsibility. You've always been the dreamer out of the two of us," he laughed affectionately. "I'm meant to be the voice of reason. I failed you, Verity."

He was still holding my hand, and I wondered if my skin was as cold from the outside as I felt on the inside.

"Unfortunately, Verity can't recall the specifics of the accident," Doctor Torres put in. "It took place in the very early hours of the morning. No hiking equipment was found."

Sebastian's eyes flashed for a moment, but his back was to the doctor, so only I saw it. He fixed his charming, appropriately pitying smile back on his face in an instant.

"Well, I'm going to fix all of this," Sebastian promised, giving my hand a gentle squeeze. "I know you've had a tough time and you're hurting, but I'm going to take care of you just like I always said I would."

God, I'd forgotten how intoxicating his confidence used to be for me. To a lonely orphan girl, he'd seemed like my salvation. My knight in shining armor. A promise that I'd never be alone again.

And when he'd changed his mind, he'd ripped all that security away from me like it was nothing, and I'd never heard from him again.

"How long until she can come home, Doctor?" Sebastian asked.

Oh fuck, that was not in my plans. No sirree. I was not going to a secondary location with this motherfucker.

Though perhaps that would give me an opening to make a run for it? I wouldn't rule it out just yet.

"We'd like to keep Verity here a little while longer, just to keep an eye on things," Doctor Torres said in a pleasant voice. "Verity, you also have a transverse fracture"—she nodded at my left arm, bound in a splint—"and some heavy bruising down your left side that's being managed with pain medication. Considering the terrain and how isolated you were... well, it was a good thing you were found quickly."

I didn't need to fake my tremulous nod this time. I was surprised I hadn't walked away with more damage, and I was counting my blessings that I hadn't.

Doctor Torres left us alone, and I kept my expression carefully blank, waiting to see what Sebastian would say now there were no witnesses around. Was this where the mask would come off? Or would he keep up the ruse?

"I've missed you," Sebastian murmured, which told me nothing at all. "I've been so worried."

"Because of the hiking trip?" I asked, giving him my most guileless expression. Man, I should have been an actress. I was fucking *nailing* this.

Or the drugs were making me think I was nailing this. But I preferred the first option.

Sebastian's brow furrowed. "Yes, of course. I never thought the hiking trip was a good idea, remember? You've never been athletically inclined," he added with a laugh.

How rude. I mean, I wasn't. Sometimes, I did yoga to make myself feel better about the utter neglect I subjected my body to, but it brought me no joy.

Some humans ran actual marathons, some humans had *Real Housewives* marathons. The universe required balance.

"But I think we've learned a lesson from this experience, hm?" Sebastian continued. Had he always been this condescending? How had I not seen it? "Once we're back home, you can focus fully on wedding planning while I'm at work. Maybe make an appointment to have that birth control removed," he added with a wink.

I laughed weakly. What the actual fuck was happening? How far was he willing to take this lie? I'd been hoping Sebastian would underestimate me, but it appeared I'd vastly underestimated *him*.

"Did your mom come with you?" I asked, attempting to look around him to the door. It wasn't like there was no precedent for it. Deb had shown up at the hospital with him when my appendix had burst, grumbling about what an inconvenience the whole thing was and how it never would have happened if I didn't consume seed oils like she was always telling me not to.

Sebastian swallowed thickly, looking down at his shiny lawyer shoes. "She passed. Six months ago."

God damn it. Did I have to act like I missed her? I wasn't sure I could pull *that* off. Meryl Streep couldn't have made that performance convincing.

"Oh. I'm sorry. I don't... remember that."

Sebastian smiled sympathetically. "No, of course not. We'll have to figure out where your memory issues begin. It seems like... a few years ago."

"*Years*? Really?" I asked, hoping I looked wide-eyed and unnerved, when mostly I was amazed at the gall of this asshole.

"We'll figure it out, Eri. Don't worry," he added hurriedly. *Eri*. God, it had been a full decade since anyone had called me that. "I imagine you're feeling quite conflicted hearing about Mom's passing. She, um, wasn't very good to you. Actually, a lot of my relationships have changed in the past few months. I didn't realize how much control she'd had over the way people saw me."

No fucking kidding.

"Did my relationships with people change too?" I asked, semi enjoying this now I was getting into character. It was like I was LARPing an alternate timeline version of my own life.

Sebastian stammered slightly before finding an answer. "Um, well, I guess you haven't been as involved with the Hunters for a while—which was Mom's fault—but you can come back now. Things have been a little up in the air recently, but they'll welcome you back. The Denver Council branch is here— they're excited to bring you home. Where you belong. Finally. And that's what I want too. Obviously. Since we're engaged."

He was beet red in the face now, and my entertainment with this whole farce increased astronomically. It was a good thing Sebastian was a deskbound property lawyer; he'd get eaten alive in a courtroom.

"Of course you want me home, we're in love," I replied with a saccharine sweet smile. "I'm just confused about why I went hiking by myself. And why I haven't been involved with the Hunters. And what did you mean by things are 'up in the air'?"

"I shouldn't have mentioned that. You're recovering. You don't need to be thinking about all that stuff right now." He'd shored himself up, and I doubted he was going to be sloppy enough to make another slip anytime soon.

Which meant there was no more benefit to be had from this conversation. I needed to reassess.

"I'm so tired," I whispered, letting my head loll weakly back onto the pillow.

"Of course." Sebastian straightened. "You're on a lot of painkillers, you need to rest. I'm staying at a motel just around the corner. Why don't I come back in a few hours? Technically, I'm still working while I'm here…"

"Sounds good." I plastered on a fake smile, trying to imagine Theon ever willingly leaving me while I was lying in a hospital bed, drugged up to my eyeballs on pain meds, and coming up short.

Sebastian stood up with a charming, soulless smile, leaning over to press his papery dry lips to my forehead. If there'd been any real food in my stomach, I'd have probably thrown up.

"I know you're hurting right now, Verity, and I wish I could take that all away. But this is a new beginning for us, okay? We're going to do things differently this time. We're going to be so happy. Letting you go... on that hiking trip, I mean"—he cleared his throat—"was the worst thing that ever happened to me. I've lived with so much regret ever since. But everything is going to be perfect from now on, okay? I love you so much. I always have."

With one last, alarmingly earnest smile, he let himself out of the room, leaving me alone.

And I realized that in all the worst-case scenarios I'd been brainstorming about his motives, I'd left out one particularly horrifying one.

Sebastian might actually *want* me back. He might actually love me, or at least think he did. His sincerity might have been real. Without the overbearing mother in his ear telling him that her precious baby boy could do better, I was suddenly not a bad option. It probably helped that he thought I had a football field-sized hole in my memories, that he could populate with whatever he wanted me to believe was real.

Not that I needed the warning bells and flashing neon light screaming 'he doesn't really love you' on repeat—I already knew that. I knew what love was. I loved Theon. There was absolutely no universe where filling his head with false memories to suit my purposes was an acceptable option, let alone the go-to.

Fuck Sebastian and his finished basement. I had a life to get back to in the shadow realm. A cat who depended on me. A husband—sort of—who I needed to feed with my super-powered vagina and stop from plotting a revolution. I was *busy*.

Now, I just needed to figure out how the hell I was going to get back home, and the sneakier the better, because this unemployed shadow duchess sure as shit didn't have health insurance, and I suspected being airlifted out of a canyon wasn't cheap.

This was bullshit. I didn't *want* to lie here like a damsel in distress, hoping Astrid would figure out a way to rescue me. I'd been nothing but a liability since I arrived in the shadow realm, and I was planning on not continuing to be a liability when I got back there. The least I could do was figure this bit out on my own.

Clinging to Sebastian like he was my lifeline would hopefully keep the senior Council members at bay, at least for a little while. They'd use him as their gofer, assuming that I'd trust him implicitly. And Sebastian, I could manage.

I tipped my head back against the pillow, smiling faintly at the memory of thinking that I could manage Theon. He was unmanageable, ungovernable, and stubborn to a fault.

And I loved him—and all of those traits he came with. Did he have a shit ton to learn about being a good mate? Yes. Though, I did too. And we definitely needed to sort out his jealousy issues when it came to Damen, though I suspected seeing me hurt would have cured him of at least some of his idiocy on that front.

The rest would come with time. I was all in on Theon, Duke of Lindow. We were going to make each other very fucking happy for the rest of our days, and no one was going to get in the way of that.

CHAPTER 20

Damen unlocked the door to my room, striding straight in without bothering to hang around in front of the bars first, his expression grim. He closed the door behind him, crossing the room to sit next to me on the bed, mirroring my posture with his back against the wall, one foot up on the edge of the mattress, and an arm resting on his knee.

Had Allerick not warned me of the possibility of this happening, Damen's solemn silence would have been alarming. I wasn't sure I'd ever seen him this serious in his life.

"Am I to go on trial then?" I asked, tipping my chin up, finding the last desperate remains of my pride.

"It's the Council of Shades," Damen replied, somewhat despairingly. "Allerick has been arguing in your favor, but they want to see you punished."

There was a brief hint of that age-old resentment I felt for Allerick flaring to life before I brushed it aside. It was instinctive at this point to blame him for my ills, but it was a reflex rather than a conviction. None of this was Allerick's doing. It was my actions that had led to Verity coming to harm, and the punishment that I myself had derived which would be my unmaking.

I climbed off the bed slowly, stretching my spine and rolling my shoulders back. "I had hoped they would hold off on a trial until Verity's return."

Damen made a quiet noise of distress. "The Councilors don't believe she will return."

"Based on what?" I asked sharply, refusing to entertain the idea that Verity would be trapped there forever. "Has Astrid changed her mind? She was confident that she would see Verity safely returned as soon as she left the healing facility."

"Well, no." Damen winced. "Astrid is as determined as ever. They think Verity will refuse to return."

"On what grounds?" I growled, shadows I didn't have the power to produce straining to break free, to lash out at *something*. Anything.

"You," Damen replied apologetically. "They're quite convinced that Verity's return to the human realm was probably a welcome getaway for her. A convenient opportunity to be rid of an unsuitable mate who'd taken her against her will."

"Verity was happy," I snarled, though my defensiveness was undeniable. I'd demanded a Hunter of my own, after all. Verity insisted she'd volunteered willingly, but she cared deeply for the other ex-Hunters who lived at Elverston House. Perhaps she *had* come willingly, but only so they didn't feel like they had to instead.

Perhaps she hadn't been happy after all, and I'd only seen what I wanted to see?

"Stop doubting yourself," Damen ordered, climbing off the bed and pulling himself up to his full height, still half a horn-length shorter than me. "I saw the two of you together the day... the day everything happened, remember? I've argued with the Councilors repeatedly, insisted that I saw the two of you happy. That *Verity* was happy. Your staff have also given their testimonials, but the Council dismissed those on the basis of bias."

"What was their excuse for dismissing yours?" I asked derisively.

"They were already not best pleased with me," Damen admitted. "Understand that while *Allerick* has been a strong proponent of allowing the ex-Hunters to find their place here—and ideally, a mate here—in their own time, not everyone agrees with his approach. The Council feel that all of the ex-Hunters should have been mated off immediately upon arrival, to ensure they would stay and produce energy for the stores. As the second in line, they have been very vocal about the fact that I should have been the second to be mated. My failure to secure a relationship has been... a cause of contention."

Unhappily, I realized that my thoughts had followed along the same lines. I'd thought that I would make a better ruler than Allerick because I would make things happen. Now, I could see that the compassion that tempered his decisions was a strength, not a weakness.

Perhaps, in a different world, we could have worked together. Our strengths may have complemented one another. It was too late now, though. Too late for the bitter and long-overdue realization that the obstacle to my own happiness had been *me* all along.

"Well, then, I suppose we've kept them waiting long enough," I sighed, clambering tiredly to my feet.

Damen jumped up with far more energy than me, standing between myself and the door, glaring at me. By the time Damen was old enough to be considered a challenger, it was clear that Allerick would surpass me. I'd never been raised alongside him as a brother, and spent even less time with him than I'd spent with a young Allerick. Sometimes, I forgot entirely that Damen *was* as much my brother as Allerick was.

He looked the very picture of an annoyed younger sibling now.

"You better not be giving up," Damen warned. "Verity is your mate. She needs you."

"Verity is always my priority," I assured him. "For as long as I live."

"Well, you're mated, so it's not like they can do anything anyway," Damen said with a dismissive flick of his hand. "The two of you are together, whether they like it or not. Verity will return, and the Councilors will learn to live with it."

Damen was young and idealistic, still—something I hadn't realized before now. Allerick clearly hadn't involved him in the less savory elements of ruling the shadow realm. He certainly hadn't told him about the punishment I was facing, perhaps to spare him from the unpleasantness of it all.

I found myself loathe to ruin his peace. Perhaps it was the same older brotherly instinct that Allerick had acted on. It was an oddly pleasing thought.

Damen let us out of the room, through the corridors that led to the curia, and I allowed myself to contemplate for the first time whether the scar of my bite would linger on Verity's skin if the Council demanded that I be returned to the shadows of the ancestors. I had no doubt that the bond would be broken and she could start over with the caliber of mate she deserved, but would a scar remain? Would she welcome the reminder of my role in her life or would she resent it?

The latter, undoubtedly.

I'd caused Verity nothing but grief in the time we'd spent together. She would probably welcome the opportunity to start over.

"You'll... you'll keep an eye on Verity, won't you?" I asked Damen hesitantly, surprised at how easy it was to make such a request without my idiotic jealousy interfering. "You'll keep her safe. If anything happens."

"Of course," he replied flippantly, not grasping the magnitude of my request.

"I mean it, Damen. See that she is kept in comfort. She drinks tea to break her fast in the morning, and doesn't like meat before midday. Her beast, Fester, must be kept indoors for his own safety, and will steal food from anyone and anything, but she cannot be without him. Verity likes a great deal of soft furnishings in her chambers—in shades of pink—and requires many beauty and comfort items from the human realm delivered regularly to her."

Damen was watching me strangely, but I forged on, needing him to know all of this. To remember it all.

"In truth, if Verity doesn't receive such items, she won't complain, as she has very low expectations of kindness and generosity, and it is imperative that you vastly exceed them, as she deserves only the best—"

Damen came to a sudden stop, holding out an arm to prevent me from going any farther, and glancing around before leaning in to speak quietly in my ear. "Maybe we should just leave?"

I choked slightly on my surprise. "Leave?"

"No one would suspect me," he added hurriedly. "It's not like you and I were ever close. It would be a risk, but I think I could get you out."

"You would do that for me?" I asked in disbelief.

"I can't listen to you speak about Verity like that, then watch you walk into that courtroom. I'm not going to pretend I always approve of your ideas, Theon, but I do think you haven't always been treated as fairly as you should have been—by Father, and the realm as a whole. You were basically banished, you never stood a chance."

"A chance of what?"

"You know." Damen gestured at me somewhat desperately. "Normalcy."

I snorted at that, some of my melancholy lifting. "Then, perhaps the realm did me a favor. I can't imagine anything more dull than being normal."

"Let's go. Let's leave," Damen urged, foolhardy and optimistic. We hadn't been close before, and he'd since been arguing my case to the King's Council by his own admission. He'd be the first and only suspect.

"It's a generous offer, Damen, but you are too valuable to risk. Someone has to look out for Verity, and I would only entrust such a task to you."

"I'm honored," he said quietly. "And I won't let you down."

"I know you won't."

Damen had a notoriously lazy reputation among the realm, but I was confident—perhaps naively—that he'd come through when it mattered.

I didn't need Damen to tell me that we were going to the largest of the rooms—the one with tiered seating for spectators. I wasn't the king or the crown prince, but I was still a blood prince of the realm. There would be an audience.

"I don't suppose I can convince you not to watch this?" I asked mildly. Damen wouldn't keep that youthful naivety for long, and I hated the thought of being the reason he lost it.

"Either we leave together or we walk in there together," he replied stubbornly, tilting his chin up in defiance.

"Then we walk in there together," I said softly, touched by the loyalty I didn't deserve.

"Last chance," Damen warned quietly as we came to a stop in front of the heavy double doors.

I grinned at him. "Until we meet again, brother."

Before he could respond, I pushed the doors open and walked into the center of the circular room, rows upon rows of Shades staring down at me from the tiered benches above.

I'd made many mistakes in my time, and now the time had come for me to answer for my crimes.

CHAPTER 21

I looked like shit.

The short walk from my bed to the bathroom had my limbs trembling, and my skin had taken on a grayish tinge. My hair had practically knitted itself together after days of wearing it down, constantly pulling it in front of the mating mark. The dark circles under my eyes seemed to grow more pronounced by the minute.

I was leaving today.

There was a bag of clothes next to the bed that Sebastian had dropped off for me yesterday that I needed to put on, and I'd come in here to pee and with the vague inclination that I should do something with my hair, but I was completely drained just from this short walk.

Which meant my half-baked plan to get lost in the crowd at the airport on the way back to Denver wasn't looking super feasible. I was in no shape to make a run for it and find myself a dark spot to wait for an assist. In my current condition, Sebastian was probably going to have to put me in a wheelchair to get through the airport.

Fuck.

I shuffled back to my bed, sweat beading on my brow from the effort. My favorite nurse, Leticia, came in while I dropped myself heavily onto the edge of the bed, trying to get my labored breathing under control.

She took in the state of me with pursed lips. "Are you in pain, Verity?"

I took stock of my body before shaking my head, grimacing. "Just tired."

Tired and *weak*. The bedrest, the injuries, and the meds had all made me feel like I'd aged thirty years in the few days I'd been here. Had this been what Theon had felt like before he'd fed? I wished sex could magically cure me.

Leticia nodded sympathetically. "I'm glad to see you up and moving around, but be aware of your limits."

"I'm very aware of them," I mumbled, reaching for my cup of water next to the bed and having a sip. My limit was a pee break. That was it.

Leticia hummed, making for the bag next to the bed. "Well, shall I help you get dressed? Your fiancé will be here soon to collect you."

I watched dispassionately as she pulled out a black business-casual dress with short sleeves, suddenly filled with flashbacks of how dull my wardrobe had been prior to the breakup. She also pulled out a pair of black pleather flats that had my nose wrinkling, both in anticipation of brutal blisters and the uniquely gross foot smell that flats produced.

Leticia barely suppressed an amused smile as she pulled out a black lace set of bra and panties, tucking her chin to hide the look on her face as she laid them on the bed next to me.

I snorted derisively, picking up the absurd scraps of fabric for closer examination. I mean, at least he'd left the tags on. They were clearly new, and not hand-me-downs from a previous lover. In fact, the bra was even in my size— though it was my size from ten years ago, so it'd be uncomfortably tight now.

Nothing creepy about that.

I pushed myself back up to standing, letting Leticia do most of the work of dressing me since my limbs were being rudely uncooperative. She made a muffled sound of discontent as she loosened the bra straps as much as possible, not that it made a difference when my cupeths overfloweth.

"It's fine," I assured her, resigned to being uncomfortable. The dress was a soft fabric at least, though it was kind of clingy, and really didn't do anything to hide the weird quadruple-boob situation the bra was giving me. The tight arm hole was also a bitch to get the splint through. Clearly, Sebastian hadn't been thinking of comfort or practicality when he'd picked these things out.

"There we go," Leticia said, straightening after helping me slip my feet into the shoes. At least they seemed to fit.

"What's this from?" Leticia murmured, tilting her head to the side to examine the bite mark that the dress's neckline wasn't quite high enough to hide.

Shit.

"You don't have to answer, I'm just being nosy," she said with a reassuring smile.

"I'm just very self-conscious about it," I replied, hoping that sounded like a believable excuse.

"I've got some foundation in my bag, if you'd like?" Leticia suggested kindly. "We're probably a pretty similar shade."

I nearly burst into tears as I nodded, giving her hand a quick squeeze of gratitude. God, nurses were so underappreciated. If I ever found my way back to the shadow realm, I was totally going to suggest some kind of elaborate headhunting scheme to the king to get Hunter medical professionals to defect to our side.

Leticia left, returning with a small makeup bag and helping me cover up the scar on my neck. It wasn't perfect, but between the foundation and my hair, I could almost get away with it.

It wasn't a long-term fix. Maybe I could convince Sebastian to stop at a drugstore? Ugh, I didn't have any money, though.

Darkness. That's what I needed. The solution was just to get the fuck out of here as soon as possible.

I gave Leticia a tight smile, hating how helpless I felt. "Thank you."

"Don't mention it. Oh, there was also a bit of a mix-up with your things," Leticia added apologetically. "This was misplaced, I just spotted it earlier."

She unfurled something from the pocket of her scrubs, holding it up for me to see. A long, thin silver chain dangled from her hand, the inky black ball of darkness held in a filigree cage swinging like a pendulum. I didn't think. I didn't hesitate. I just snatched it out of her grasp instantly, all but cradling it to my chest.

"It's very pretty," Leticia murmured. "I've never seen anything quite like it."

I made some kind of sound of agreement, blinking back a sudden rush of tears, running my thumb over the filigree casing that housed the small glass orb. It looked different in this realm, unless my eyes were playing tricks on me.

Which, you know, head injury. So maybe.

But I was sure it hadn't been so... *active* when Theon had shown it to me.

"Was it a gift from your fiancé?"

"What?" I blinked up at her. "Oh. Um, sure. Yeah."

She hummed, watching me a little too closely. "You know, Verity, if there's anything you'd like to talk about, I'm always here."

Maybe my amnesia act wasn't totally working on the actual medical professional. Leticia and Doctor Torres seemed nice, but the reach of the Hunters was long and their pockets were deep. I couldn't trust that they wouldn't report back if I asked for help.

God, it was tempting though. I wasn't someone who thrived on my own. I, much like an infant, needed a village to support me. The past few days had been fucking terrifying.

"Think about it," Leticia said with a kind smile. She let the subject drop as she went through her routine checks, keeping the conversation light while she inspected the splint on my arm before excusing herself from the room.

Sebastian's charming laugh echoed down the hall as he made small talk with the nurses, and I realized with a jolt that I still had the necklace in my hand. This stupid dress had no pockets, and if Sebastian saw the chain around my neck, he'd definitely want to know what it was and where I got it.

Panicking slightly, I shoved it down my dress, tucking it into the bottom of my bra cup, hoping the boob squish would hide any lumps. My eyes watered slightly at the feeling of the metal digging into my flesh, but at least it was hidden.

"There you are, Eri," Sebastian said, spreading his arms wide as he entered the room, giving me a magnanimous smile. "You look... lovely. Perhaps you could tie your hair up? Ah, never mind. We can deal with it later. Let's get out of here, hm?"

I exhaled heavily, giving him what I hoped was a convincing smile.

As sorry for myself as I was feeling, this wasn't the time to indulge my own self-pity. Now was the time to channel my inner Astrid and think strategically about how I was going to get the hell out of here.

The tears would have to wait a little longer.

"I thought we were going home?" My heart started pounding uncomfortably fast in my chest as Sebastian pulled the rental car up to the swirly gates of an absurdly large mansion. This wasn't the airport. We were meant to be going back to Denver. That's what he'd said.

He shot me a reassuring smile that looked a little strained around the edges as he lowered the window to reach the buzzer. "Just a quick pit stop on the way. A lot of the Council flew in because they were so worried about you, Eri. The least we can do is say hello, don't you think?"

The rebuke in his voice was clear. Not wanting to risk messing up now, I shrank down in my seat, giving him the small, hesitant nod of agreement he was searching for. I alarmed myself with how easily I was able to slip back into that version of me from ten years ago. I hated that I'd ever forced myself to be so small so that Sebastian could take up all of the space for both of us.

The journey from who I'd been then to who I was now hadn't necessarily been one of conscious, intentional change. It had just been one day of freedom at a time. One day of not having to hide what I'd always considered the ugly parts of myself at a time. And with each day that passed, the guilt and shame I'd always carried around lessened until it was just a distant memory.

That fateful afternoon in my bedroom, Deb had told me I was broken, but now I was banishing her proclamation from my mind for good. I wasn't fundamentally broken—no one was—and I deserved love. I deserved to be loved, with all of my oddities, and my too-loud voice, and my sometimes inappropriate jokes.

I wanted that someone who loved me to be Theon. And I wanted to be the someone who loved him. Who showed him that there was good in the world he'd been avoiding for so long. Who encouraged his incredible experiments, and ate lunch with him each day, and kept him strong and healthy with the power I gave him.

And Theon wasn't the only reason I needed to get home. The house was too big for Wilder and Aderith to manage alone. I wanted to take on some of their workload, make the manor a nicer place for all of us to live. I wanted to spend more time with bright and cheery Xanthia, and find a way to win over Rainy.

I wasn't broken. It had just taken me a while to realize that all the parts that made up who I was were pieces of an interesting puzzle, not a mess of unwanted scraps.

The gates opened, and we headed up the semicircular driveway that led to the elegant gray-brick colossus that we were apparently visiting. The driveway was packed with vehicles, and I arranged my face into something faintly apprehensive as Sebastian parked. I was going into the heart of the viper's nest, I needed to have my wits about me. If ever I needed to be underestimated, now was the time.

I wrapped my good arm around my middle, embracing the feeling of the necklace digging into my skin for a moment, anchoring me in reality. I didn't belong here. This was no longer my world.

I was going to find my way into the dark, and Theon would come for me. The mating bond in my chest was muffled, but it was there. He would come for me.

For my own sanity, I had to believe that I meant as much to Theon as he meant to me.

Sebastian headed around the front of the vehicle to open my door for me, standing back while I unbuckled and climbed out on my own. When we'd been together, I hated how little he seemed to want to touch me outside of sex, it had always made me feel so unwanted. I couldn't be more glad for it now.

"What am I meant to say to them?" I asked, giving Sebastian my best Bambi eyes again. "I've never gone in front of the Council before."

That much was true. I'd been a pretty mediocre Hunter before I'd been booted out, with no kills to my name. I doubted any of the higher-ups had ever heard my name before Deb had dragged it through the mud.

Sebastian grabbed my good hand, giving it an unwanted squeeze. "Just whatever you can remember, Eri. I'll be right beside you the whole time, okay?"

Lucky me.

But this was better than facing them alone, I reminded myself. This was the reason I'd wanted Sebastian here in the first place. Those assholes actually respected him.

Fortunately, there was only one step up to the expansive porch that led to the front door, because even that was enough to jostle my already aching bones. The front door swung open before we could knock, a portly, balding man ushering us inside with a smile that didn't reach his eyes.

"Welcome, welcome. So good to see you up and about, Verity. My name is Samuel Winston, I'm a member of the Utah branch of the Hunters Council, and this is my home. I'm so glad you could come by."

"Thank you." I didn't have to fake shrinking in on myself this time. I was flailing around *way* out of my depth.

"Come, come, let's join the others." Samuel led us into an absurdly large beige living room, dominated by a red velvet sectional and a grand piano. There were people *everywhere*, some whom I vaguely recognized, and others I didn't.

Fuck, fuck, fuck.

Maybe I'd overestimated my ability to handle this.

My gaze settled on Lucas from the hospital, standing half-concealed behind the piano and looking wildly uncomfortable. Good. It was his fault all these people knew where I was in the first place, I hoped both sides of his pillow were warm for the rest of his life.

"Verity." A woman stepped forward who I *did* recognize—Moriah Nash, a member of the Colorado Council. She'd always intimidated me, and not just because of prestigious position. It was probably the severe silvery-black bob that did it. Combined with the black turtleneck, she was really embracing the kids-movie-villain aesthetic. "You look tired. Come, let's go sit in the kitchen, it's very crowded in here, isn't it? Sebastian, why don't you stay here?"

His hand tightened around mine. "I think it would be best if I stayed with her."

Huh. That was more spine than he'd shown in our entire five-year relationship.

Moriah's eyes narrowed, though her plastic smile stayed fixed in place. "Of course. Come through this way. Samuel has been very kind to let us use his home as a meeting place for the past few days."

It's not like he can't spare the space, I thought wryly as we entered the kitchen, noting that there were seven heavy wooden barstools arranged around the kitchen island and it didn't feel crowded.

Sebastian helped me up onto the corner stool, taking the one beside me and draping his arm along the back of my seat. Moriah watched every movement with hawklike intensity as she took her own seat, angling herself to face me.

"First, tell me how you're feeling, Verity?" she began, folding her hands in her lap. "We've all been so worried since you've been away."

"On my hiking trip?" I asked, blinking heavily.

Moriah gave me an unsettling smile. "Now, you mustn't be mad at Sebastian, but he did tell you a little white lie on that front. We felt it was for your own good as you were in the hospital and dealing with human medical professionals, we didn't want you to get confused and say something that may alarm them."

"Oh?" I glanced back at Sebastian, who was staring guiltily at the granite countertop. Maybe this terrible pit stop would have its uses after all. Maybe I could learn something valuable to take back with me.

Moriah touched my hand, drawing my attention back to her, and I did my best not to flinch.

"In truth," she began with a sigh. "You were kidnapped by the Shades, and held in the shadow realm for some months against your will."

I gasped quietly at this. Maybe I should faint? Swoon off the barstool?

Moriah nodded gravely. "We believe they assaulted you, and left you in the desert for dead."

Fuck, it was hard not to object to that. On the plus side, I could finally let the tears I'd been holding back for days fall in earnest.

Fortunately, Sebastian was immensely out of his element when it came to crying women, and made no attempt to comfort me.

"It was very difficult for me to tell you this," Moriah—the true victim, apparently—sighed. "But it would be cruel to let you believe a lie any longer."

The stone-cold audacity.

"You were a victim of the escalating war between Hunters and Shades. They have gotten increasingly bold, even dragging humans into it with their puppet, Austin Thibaut."

I could imagine Austin throwing his head back and laughing when he heard that, and it made me feel substantially better.

"It is essential that if you have *any* recollections of your time in the shadow realm, that you tell us. We must know what they're planning, Verity. How can we defend ourselves against it otherwise? How can we keep the human population safe?"

"Eri will tell me anything that she remembers," Sebastian said firmly. "But she needs to rest. The priority needs to be on her recovery right now."

"Naturally," Moriah agreed smoothly, eyes flashing with irritation. "Which is why you'll stay here for the next few days. There is plenty of space, and Verity is safely surrounded by people who care about her well-being. The lights are on at all times, and there are no switches in the rooms so they can't be tampered with. You are entirely safe from monstrous shadow creatures here."

Was that a threat or a promise?

"Thank you," I murmured, rubbing my temples dramatically.

"I'll show you to the room we have set aside for you," Moriah announced, the scrape of the stool on the tile making me wince. "Perhaps after a few hours' rest, you'll be able to join us for dinner. We're all here to see *you*, after all."

"Perhaps," I agreed, mortified at the very thought.

It was a painfully slow journey upstairs to a small guest bedroom, and I all but collapsed on the dark gray brocade comforter, my limbs shaking with the effort of climbing up the stairs.

"Sebastian," Moriah clipped. "Why don't you return downstairs with me and we'll get Verity some water?"

That definitely wasn't a two-person job. I suspected he hadn't played his part quite the way they had planned, and was about to get raked over the coals for it. He would probably return far pushier for information, which was going to be annoying.

Before I could decide how to handle that, the door opened again. I lifted my head feebly, expecting to see Sebastian, but finding a panicked-looking Lucas standing in front of it instead, breathing heavily.

"Tell me it's not terrible there."

"What?" I asked, blinking at him.

"The shadow realm. Tell me it's not actually awful. That they treated you well. That women who go there are safe."

I dropped my head back to the mattress. "Sorry. I've got amnesia."

"No, you don't. I'm not messing around, if it's not safe, then I need to stop her. Hurry, before your stupid fake boyfriend gets back."

"That's rude." I stared up at the ceiling, contemplating my options. The shadow realm *was* safe so long as whoever he'd sent on their way didn't mean any harm. If they wanted to defect, they'd be welcome. I wasn't about to drop my ruse for Lucas's benefit when he'd been the one to call the cavalry on me in the first place.

He made a noise of frustration, letting himself out of the room, and I kicked off my shoes and crawled up the bed, huddling under the comforter and feigning sleep in the hopes that Sebastian would leave me alone.

It seemed to work. He quietly set down a glass of water on the nightstand before leaving again, the door clicking shut behind him. Were there cameras in here? Maybe. Probably.

Shit. Now what was I meant to do? After a few minutes, I gave up lying still and sat up to have some water, looking around the room. There appeared to be a half bathroom attached, and I climbed out of bed, padding across the room and sliding the pocket door closed behind me.

True to Moriah's words, there was no light switch in the tiny bathroom. I leaned over the sink, splashing my face with water to wake myself up, and drying off before reaching down my dress to fish the necklace out of my bra and give my aching boob a break.

Entranced by the swirling motion, I undid the clasp holding the cage together, letting the orb roll into my hand. The way it moved was fascinating. I was sure I'd remember if it had been swirling this fast back in Theon's workshop.

Caspite.

"It is more like... living darkness, I suppose. It expands, takes over everything it can." That was how he'd described it. Like the in-between was stuck in place, but it if it could spread farther it would, except it couldn't survive outside of its environment. I pulled the silver chain over my head, my fingers closed around the glass, clutching it tightly in my good hand as a slightly deranged idea began to form.

It probably wasn't going to work.

And then I'd also be sans beautiful orb for my necklace.

But it was also a chance.

And *not* having the orb might be a good thing. The silver necklace on its own was easier to explain away if any of the Hunters saw it.

I could hear murmurings and the odd burst of laughter from downstairs, and the idea of going back there and facing that crowd again made me nauseous. The idea of Sebastian holding my hand again made me feel nauseous.

The idea of sitting around, hoping that Theon hadn't forgotten about me, that Astrid was finding a way to save me, made me feel worse than those things combined. I didn't want to be a burden on them.

I had to do my part to find my way home too.

I turned with a trembling exhale, leaning back against the basin, and threw the orb with all my strength against the beige tile wall opposite. The glass shattered, and a black sludge-like substance slid down the wall, small and insignificant. Just a small dollop of mystery goop that I was going to have to explain away that had done nothing.

I slumped against the sink, my throat burning as I tried to hold back tears. It had been a long shot anyway. What had I really expected?

The inky sludge pooled at the baseboard, and just as I was wondering how I was supposed to clean up this foreign substance before the Hunters put me on a torture rack, it started to expand, coating the floor in a layer of black before climbing up the walls, and spidering over the off-white ceiling, completely concealing the fluorescent lighting and encasing the room in darkness.

My breath was sawing in my lungs, far too loud in the perfect silence as the room vanished around me. Hesitantly, I took a step forward, followed by another. Was there enough space in here for this to work? I reached my shaking hands out in front of me, waiting to hit a wall at the far end of the bathroom, and finding only air. Somewhat bolstered and mostly terrified, I took a stumbling step forward. And then another. And then another.

"Hello?" I called out tentatively, giving my eyes a moment to adjust. The portals were still active on the Shade side. If I kept walking, I had to find one eventually, right? Right. Or I'd run into someone in the in-between, and hopefully, they were nice.

It wasn't my most solid plan, but I'd committed now. Shit, I really hoped that portal sludge disintegrated on its own. I did not need a herd of Hunters following me here.

Bolstered by the idea of getting away from them, I trudged on into nothingness. Oddly, I didn't feel particularly strongly either way about the fact that I would never see Sebastian again. I thought I'd be thrilled, but by the end of it all... I just felt *nothing* where he was concerned, except for maybe a vague hope that he'd leave the Hunters someday and choose a better life for himself.

I peered into the darkness, calling out again to try to get someone's attention. Nothing lived in the in-between, right? Like creatures and such? No, surely not.

Someone would have definitely mentioned that.

Maybe.

"Hiiiiiiii," I called breathily, panting slightly. The pain meds were doing their job for now, but they'd wear off, and I didn't have any more. I should have put my smelly flats back on. The ground was freezing cold and unforgivingly hard beneath my bare feet. "Is anyone else in here?"

Nothing. There was no echo either, nothing to give me any idea of space or structure. My words just hit the emptiness and died on impact, barely carrying. My footsteps were almost soundless, despite my heavy, limping gait. Shades had good night vision, but I really needed to make at least a little bit of noise to draw attention to my presence if they were farther away.

"*But I would walk five hundred miles,*" I began pant-singing, since I had walking on my mind. "*And I would walk five hundred more...*"

I'm going to be falling down at your door, Theon.

You'd better be ready to pick me back up again.

VERITY

CHAPTER 22

I'd never noticed it before, but the ground of the in-between was *so* cold. Hard, too. I felt like I was lying on a slab of frigid marble, and I desperately wanted to get to my feet, but the rest of my body wasn't cooperating with that idea.

I didn't want to believe that I was going to die here, alone in the dark, so close and yet so far from where I was running to. But I was.

The bond was a weak, fading pulse in my chest, dying right along with me.

Would Theon move on? Find another Hunter mate to replace me with? He'd told me that he was more attached to me than he expected to be, and I'd read so much into that. Now, I was less certain.

But I was dying, so perhaps it was a blessing that he didn't love me the way I loved him. I didn't want him to suffer any more than necessary.

For a long while, I alternated between dozing and shivering, hating the sensation of being awake. My voice was too hoarse to so much as whisper, so I didn't even have the luxury of distracting myself by singing. My memories were a beautiful solace, though. In the peaceful sanctuary of my mind, I was at home with Theon. I was at Lindow, and the rain I'd come to love fell constantly, a comforting drip, drip, drip against the stone while we were warm and dry inside. The library was clear of dust, and we were sweaty and satisfied, tangled up in each other while Fester prowled the estate, searching for scraps of meat to steal. Rainy was tucked up in her bedroom—surly but safe—and Aderith and Wilder were sharing tea and cake by the fireplace downstairs.

It was a mash-up of memories, coated in a filmy haze of wishful thinking, and yet it felt so tangible that I could almost touch it. The pitter-patter of the rain; the warm, solid bulk of Theon's body at my back; the smell of sex and the citrusy cleaner Aderith used to scrub the floors in the dining room; the gentle hum of voices from around the estate.

What a beautiful life we could have had. What a perfect dream to carry me into whatever came next. I clung to it with everything I had as I was carried away into the next life, the journey far less gentle than I expected it to be.

It was rushed, and I was jostled, and there was shouting. So much shouting.

This was not the peaceful, pearlescent afterlife I'd been told about.

"Verity!"

I winced at the sound of my name so close to my ear. Strange that it sounded like Tallulah's voice, though. Was she dead too? I hoped not.

Instead of the solid, jostling beneath me, there was a soft bed. And then a cold, wet cloth swiping over my face, making me squirm to try get away from the horrid sensation.

And with dawning realization, and a mixture of relief and a little bit of dread, I understood that I wasn't dead.

I wasn't dead.

My body felt fucking awful, and I couldn't imagine ever *not* feeling awful again, but I was alive.

"You're awake," Meera whispered, sniffling. "Here, have some water. You look parched."

I groaned as someone raised me into a sitting position and the cool edge of a cup was pressed to my lips. At the first taste of water, I tried to gulp down the whole lot, not realizing how thirsty I'd actually been until I started.

"Slowly," Meera said softly, pulling the cup away. "You'll make yourself sick. What hurts? What do you need? God, we've been so worried about you—"

"Theon," I rasped, squinting against the light in the room as I forced my eyes open. "Where's Theon?"

Meera and Tallulah exchanged a loaded look that had the cobwebs clearing from my brain faster than anything else could have.

"Where's Theon?" I asked harshly, struggling to get out of bed even though my legs felt like they were made of water. Had he not made it back from the human realm? What if a Hunter had gotten him after I'd passed out? No, I'd know, right? The bond felt so weak and threadbare in my chest that it was practically nonexistent, but it wasn't *gone*.

"You're going to hurt yourself," Tallulah fussed, gently trying to push me back into bed. "He's... well, he's on trial."

"*What*?!"

"Evrin has already sent a guard ahead to tell them you're back, in case they want to delay—"

I didn't wait for Tallulah to finish, I was already up, stumbling for the door in my bare feet. I wasn't even entirely sure where I was, it wasn't somewhere I recognized.

"We'll ask them to delay the trial until you're better," Tallulah said worriedly, wrapping an arm around my waist. "It's been going for *hours* already. Verity, you're not up to this. You can barely stand."

"I don't care about that! I need to get to Theon!"

What kind of trial? Was he frightened? He didn't have a large support system. I didn't even know if Rainy had made it back, and Xanthia would be beside herself if she hadn't, and in no state to be there for her son. He needed me.

"She's not going to be talked out of this," Meera said smoothly. "Verner, are you still there?" she called through the door.

Verner—the guard that was always following Meera around with a longing look on his face—appeared instantly, as though he'd been waiting for her summons.

"Can you carry Verity?"

I was already making grabby hands for him because I felt about two seconds away from collapsing.

"Wait," Tallulah said, letting Verner steady me and pulling off her cherry red coat. "Put this on, you're shivering. What are you even going to do?" she asked, guiding my arms into the sleeves.

Meera watched me with assessing eyes. "I think we're going to go make a scene."

"Fuck yes, we are," I rasped, my head spinning slightly at the effort of standing on my own two feet.

Surprisingly, Meera seemed to be more enthusiastic about this plan than Tallulah was, but I got the impression that Tallulah *really* liked rules.

That wasn't something we had in common. Rules were meant to be broken, and my mate wasn't meant to be on trial.

Theon thought of himself as the villain in Allerick's story, but he was the hero in mine. And sometimes, heroes needed to be rescued too.

Verner had led us through a maze of corridors that were exclusively for the guards to use, staring down any of the Guard who looked like they were going to object.

One member of the Guard was brave enough to approach, jogging up to us and giving me a slightly alarmed look. "You're awake?"

"This is Evrin," Tallulah mumbled. "He was the one who found you in the in-between. You were right outside the portal, you know. So close."

I swallowed thickly, nodding at Evrin in gratitude. "Did they pause the trial?"

He grimaced. "My message was only conveyed to the Councilors, not announced to the room. They refused to delay."

The sound of raised voices filtered through the door, and to my surprise, I realized that the one shouting was *Damen*.

"I need to get in there," I demanded. If Damen was shouting at my mate, I was going to have serious fucking words with the crown prince.

Only *I* got to tell Theon off, and I had a list of complaints, starting with how dare he make me fall in love with him.

I basically threw myself out of Verner's arms the moment the door was open, stumbling into a circular room with rows of benches filled with Shades staring down at me, and the four uncertain ex-Hunters and Shades that made up my little crew.

But I didn't care about them. I walked with all the grace of a baby deer into the center of the room, my gaze transfixed on Theon. He dashed toward me with a pained sound, catching me in his arms before I hit the ground and pulling me in tight. The room disappeared around me as I shoved my face into his chest, inhaling the scent of him that I'd missed so much, wetting his skin with my tears. That I wasn't instantly cocooned in shadows showed how hungry Theon was, though I didn't think I had enough in the tank for him to even feed from right now.

If I did, he'd be getting a blowjob in front of all these stuffy assholes staring down at us, their opinions be damned.

"What is going on? Why are you here?" I asked, sniffling into Theon's front. Someone was ordering me to move back, that I wasn't allowed to be here, but I could already hear Damen yelling at them, so I ignored it.

Perhaps he hadn't been telling off Theon. Perhaps he'd been defending him.

"Never mind that. You're hurt. You need medical attention, they shouldn't have brought you here." Theon ran his hands carefully over everywhere he could reach without letting go of me, assessing every injury for himself. "Your scent…"

"I missed you," I whispered uncertainly, the chill of rejection running down my spine. Maybe he didn't want me here. I was the reason he was being put through this stupid trial in the first place.

"My love, life has not been worth living without you. But your health is more important to me than my selfish desire to see you."

It was everything I wanted to hear, but there was more to it.

"What aren't you telling me?"

Theon hesitated, but before I could warn him not to lie, Allerick was there, speaking a truth too horrible to bear.

"The Council of Shades has found Theon guilty of the abduction of a protected ex-Hunter of this realm. They have sentenced him to death by a thousand silver blades."

"What? No."

I tried to spin around to face Allerick, but Theon held me firmly in place, gently guiding my chin up so my gaze met his.

"No," I said forcefully, wishing my voice didn't sound so shaky. "No. I don't accept that. I'm here. I'm fine. Theon didn't abduct me—"

He made a sound of disagreement, and I all but growled at him like a feral hyena. "I volunteered to go to Lindow with you!"

"The abduction in question refers to him claiming you as a mate against your will," Allerick murmured. "The charge is enough on its own to warrant death, without taking into consideration your injuries, and the unsanctioned trip to the human realm—"

"I fell," I shot back stubbornly. "Theon, you can't seriously be going along with this shit. This whole thing is a joke."

"Perhaps you could give your version of events to the Councilors, Verity," Damen suggested loudly. "I'm *sure* they will be willing to listen, given that Verity's well-being is the subject of this entire farce. I know I've given my testimony loudly and repeatedly about my experience of seeing the two of you the day after he gave you the mating mark."

I startled at that, but the tone of Damen's voice seemed to suggest he was on our side. I wasn't entirely confident that I *had* made a good impression that first morning, but perhaps I was wrong.

"Of course." I went to turn in Theon's arms, still relying on his body to keep me upright, but his grip tightened just enough to keep me in place.

"Verity, you don't need to do this. You can be free. You can start over."

My jaw dropped at the frankly audacious suggestion.

"I dragged myself through hell to get back to you," I said fiercely, poking him in the chest. "I refuse to live in a world without you in it. If you think you just get to up and die and leave me here, you are very fucking mistaken, *Your Grace*. You belong to me, and I'm not letting you go."

He gave me a long look, searching my expression. He was so cocky, that sometimes it was hard to remember there were a lot of insecurities beneath all that bluster.

There was more I wanted to say. Words I wanted to give him.

But not here.

Theon had already given so much of his life, of his privacy, to the realm. I didn't want him to have to share this too.

That moment was for us.

He nodded once, straightening to survey the Council, his gloriously haughty demeanor firmly back in place.

There we go. Theon, Duke of Lindow, was back and ready to talk some shit. Bolstered by his confidence, I spun—almost keeling over entirely—back around in his arms to face the Councilors, staring them down despite their height advantage.

"What have you to say for yourself then?" one of the Councilors asked with a resigned sigh, glancing nervously around the increasingly agitated crowd.

"Simply, that Theon is mine and I'm his. That he recognized that from the very first night together and claimed me as such, but I knew it earlier. I'm impulsive, sure, but I've actually dated pretty cautiously since I arrived in the shadow realm. It took me a while to feel comfortable with any of the Shades here. Ask Rigel—" Theon made a grumbling sound of discontent at my back and I barely held back an affectionate eye roll. "Why was I so comfortable with him? He looked frail, yes, but I knew he wouldn't always. It was just... him. There was something about Theon that called to me."

"Perhaps his peculiarities called to yours," one of the Councilors suggested in such a mild tone that I couldn't decide if it was meant to be an insult or not.

"Well, I *know* that's true," I conceded. "Though, it was more than that. Perhaps, it was that I felt like I was aimlessly floating around here. I wasn't *needed* the way that the other ex-Hunters seemed to be needed in order to make the realm a more hospitable place for our kind, because I had no skills to value. But Theon..." I shrugged, my throat tight. "Theon needed me. And I needed him, I just didn't realize it right away."

The crowd's murmurs grew louder, pointed comments being directed the way of the Councilors that they clearly didn't appreciate. I narrowed my eyes, considering for the first time that maybe this wasn't about us necessarily, or even about Theon's recent actions. This was about power, and Theon's place within the shadow realm as a whole.

"Here's the deal," I began, letting the thoughts flow directly from my brain to my mouth without examining them first. It was a risky strategy. "Is Theon, Duke of Lindow, a little crazy? Hell yes. Wouldn't you be? He was raised to be one thing most of his life, paraded around in front of you to be loved and adored, then thrown away and forgotten about. I challenge you all to think about *one* person in your life who disregarded you, and how shitty it made you feel, then imagine that feeling on a realm-wide scale."

I paused to catch my breath, glaring at all the uncomfortable Shades in the crowd. *Good.* I hoped they felt bad.

"I don't think this trial is about *me* or *us* at all. I think it's about him, and I think it's about *you*. Because you don't know what to do with him. You've made him into a villain because you need to *put* him somewhere in your minds—the former prince who you all fawned over, then threw away. It's such a waste, too. Theon is *brilliant*. He could have been such an asset to the realm, if you weren't so shortsighted."

"You seemed very fond of his suggested punishments for Shades who wronged ex-Hunters," Allerick agreed wryly. Granted, the king wasn't super expressive at the best of times, but I relaxed infinitesimally at his calm demeanor. Surely, that meant that he wouldn't *actually* let Theon be executed.

"If you're hoping your words would indemnify the Duke of Lindow—" a Councilor began.

"I'm not done talking yet," I snapped, gripping Theon's forearms tightly like someone would snatch him away from my back at any moment. "Theon is the only reason I made it back."

"Theon has been held at the Pit or under direct supervision the entire time you've been gone," the Councilor shot back, a lot grumpier now. Apparently, he wasn't a fan of my snippy attitude.

Well, I wasn't a fan of his obnoxious one either.

I fished the chain of the now purely decorative necklace out from beneath Tallulah's coat, the cage dangling open as I held it up for the spectators to see.

"It's empty now, but this cage held a glass ball of the pure essence of the in-between." Murmurs broke out among the crowd, and I raised my voice so they would be able to hear me over the noise. "Honey, tell them what it was," I said, elbowing Theon gently.

"Caspite."

"Right, caspite. Theon created this himself. He found a way to contain the in-between in a tiny ball, and it saved my life when I needed to escape. It operated as a portal all on its own once I smashed it."

Theon's arms tightened around me, his voice barely a whisper against the shell of my ear. "My clever mate. I had no idea it would do such a thing."

I almost preened. I'd been called many things in my life, but I'd never been called *clever*.

"If you can't see the potential this has, you're being willfully ignorant," I told the Councilors, channeling my inner duchess and looking down my nose at them. "*This* is the key you've been missing. *This* is the way to circumvent the Hunters Council's restriction on portals, and allow those who wish to leave the Hunters to come here."

The noise of the crowd was so loud that I could barely make out a few of the Council's weak objections over it. They were grasping at straws, claiming that it would allow anyone to come to the shadow realm. That actually it was a *bad* thing.

"The Hunters *Council* and those loyal to them control access to the portals. They're the ones who wish you harm, and they can already come here," Allerick pointed out impatiently. "It's those who *don't* have a way out who are limited by portal access."

"Surely, you're not worried about the ability of the Shades to defend their realm against Hunters?" I taunted, though it was a challenge rooted in truth.

Rainy was a teenager and she could gut me with her claws or shred me with her teeth, without expending any of her power. Not to mention the restraints and weapons their shadow magic could create.

"Theon's creation took Verity to the in-between," Allerick said, the crowd calming to listen to him. "That is still our first line of defense, and can be easily bolstered. We've been too lax on our security there for too long anyway."

"Is that your official position on this, Your Majesty?" a member of the Council demanded, glaring at Allerick.

Allerick gave him a look that would have had me fighting, flighting, fawning, and freezing all at once.

"It is. Theon went against my edict, and a suitable punishment will need to be decided upon. But that suitable punishment is not death." The king turned to face me, his expression infinitely patient. "As you were the abducted one, Verity, why don't you determine what a suitable punishment is?"

This set off a whole new round of spluttering and objections from the high table, which Allerick quelled with another fearsome look.

I straightened as much as I could while my head was swimming and my legs were threatening to give out at any moment. "Theon should work with King Allerick, Captain Soren, Astrid, and whoever else needs to be involved to create a supply of these orbs." I paused for a moment. Theon exhaled heavily behind me as though this was the worst thing he'd ever heard. "He's also got a bunch of other great inventions in progress, so really you should just employ him on a permanent basis. I can assure you, he will find this to be an acute sort of torture, and consider it a punishment for the rest of his days."

"You have no idea," Theon sighed in my ear. "But if it means keeping you, then there's no punishment I wouldn't face. Come on, Allerick can sort out the details. We're going home, and I'm dragging every healer I can find with us."

CHAPTER 23

The journey from the curia back to Lindow passed in a blur. I carried Verity the entire way, a large retinue of her friends and the palace healers following in my wake.

"What do you need?" I asked Verity in a low voice, lifting her up a little higher so her face was closer to mine, needing to feel her breath on my skin. She looked so fragile, her arm was in some kind of contraption that limited its movement, and there were dark marks beneath her eyes that I'd never seen before.

"Sleep. Water. Food. You. Not in that order." She punctuated her words with a yawn, and Meera rattled off instructions to one of the Guard, ordering them back to the palace to fetch human food.

"Should someone get Astrid and Soren?" Tallulah asked, sounding nervous to speak up in such a crowd. "They're in the human realm, right? By the hospital?"

"I'll go," one of the Guard said, breaking off from the crowd.

"Astrid is going to be so mad at you," Ophelia said to my mate, jogging to keep up with the pace I was setting. "It's how you know she cares."

Verity laughed weakly, leaning her head against my shoulder. I was trying to show solicitude for my mate's friends to prove that I was worthy of her affections, but it was an immense task. I was quite ready to tell the lot of them to fuck off so I could be alone with her.

Verity wouldn't like it. She's been through enough. Don't make things harder for her.

Wilder and Aderith met us at the doors, ushering us in with looks of concern and relief.

"I'm taking you to my room," I told Verity gruffly. "You sleep there now."

In my mind, the words had sounded more like a request.

"Can I use the mistress dungeon as a walk-in wardrobe?" Verity asked hopefully.

I didn't know what that was. "Yes. Whatever you like."

"Is there anything you would deny me right now?" Verity laughed, turning her head to brush a light kiss over my shoulder.

"Time away from me."

Verity's scent sweetened, her expression softening. "I don't want that either." She used her arm around my neck to pull herself up, wincing at the effort, but making a sound of disagreement when I attempted to shift her back down.

Verity's lips brushed the shell of my ear, her voice so quiet I could barely hear her over the sound of my footsteps. "I'm in love with you, Theon, Duke of Lindow."

I closed my eyes for a brief moment, savoring the utter perfection of those words. "I'm in love with you too, Verity, Duchess of Lindow. I am never letting you go."

"You're quite sure she's okay?" I asked Aderith, picking up the orb I'd been working on before setting it down again. "Maybe I should go back up there—"

Aderith gave me an impatient look, far more confident with me now than she'd ever dared to be in the past. "If I may be blunt, Your Grace—"

"Theon," I corrected gruffly, not for the first time. It was an adjustment for all of us.

"Theon." Aderith conceded with a tilt of her chin. "If I may be blunt, the mistress of the house has requested a break from your hovering."

I scoffed. "She's had a break."

Aderith threw her hands up in exasperation. "Wait until Meera has gone, at least. You make her nervous."

That was harder to argue with. Meera was removing the splint from Verity's arm today, having visited most days for weeks to attend to my mate. Of the ex-Hunters, she appeared to have the most knowledge of medical matters, though she continuously insisted she didn't have any experience in this particular arena.

Not wanting her to risk making a mistake while tending to my mate, I stayed put in my workshop, preparing what I needed to show Allerick when he visited tomorrow. He'd deferred the start of my sentence while Verity recovered, but she'd primly told Ophelia on the queen's last visit that she was more than ready for me to start my punishment, little wretch that she was. *My* little wretch, who I loved more than anyone in this realm or any other.

How long had it been? Surely, I'd been down here long enough by now. It was nearly time for our midday meal. Did my mate expect me to eat without her? The idea was unthinkable.

Outraged at the very idea of taking our meals separately, I began marching upstairs to tell my mate as such, pausing midstep when I felt a shift in the bond.

She was moving.

The incessant noise in my mind, the unending worry that never seemed to end, ceased. My world narrowed down to my basest instincts as I tracked my prey through the corridors, the many newly opened rooms offering plenty of places for my mate to hide.

She hadn't gone into any of those, though.

No, my sentimental little mate wanted a repeat of last time. I followed the steps she'd taken up to the third floor, keeping my footfall silent as I crept through the halls, ducking into the narrow servants' corridor and slipping the hidden panel in the library wall open so I could duck into the room unseen.

Verity huffed in frustration as she searched the room for me, her chest heaving in the skintight dark pink scrap of fabric she'd been running around in.

She *looked* well. And she certainly *smelled* well. Her arm was free of the splint it had been in for the past few weeks. The rich, luxurious scent of her desire filled the room. Still, a voice in the back of my mind protested at the idea of playing these games together.

She was still recovering.

She'd been gravely injured.

It was *my* fault she was gravely injured.

I hesitated, my cock straining beneath my shadows. I had to be the sensible one here. I couldn't risk bringing my mate—my *heart*—to harm again.

Verity narrowed her eyes, her hands coming to rest petulantly on her hips. "You better not be hiding in a corner hesitating because you think I can't handle this."

I only just hid my amused snort. Verity knew me better than I knew myself.

"Oh, you are, aren't you?" She sighed dramatically. "Get out here and take your punishment."

That piqued my curiosity. "I thought my punishment was working for the king."

Verity whirled around, squinting between the shelves in my direction.

"That was your restitution to the *realm*."

I swallowed thickly, stepping into her line of sight. "Of course, my love. You should punish me as you see fit. For the rest of my days."

Verity rolled her eyes. "You don't even know what you're in trouble for. But you're not allowed to come. You're going to give me so many orgasms that I can't see straight and then you're going to carry me back to bed and snuggle me, and you're not going to come."

I groaned, my knot throbbing in anticipation.

"Lift me onto the table, please," Verity requested imperiously. Unable to deny her anything, I placed her carefully on the edge of the grand table. With no preamble, she lay back on her elbows, bending her legs and spreading them apart, revealing her bare cunt beneath the tight dress.

"You've been running around the manor like this?" I growled, dropping heavily to my knees and pressing her legs farther apart.

"I told everyone to stay downstairs," Verity replied breathily.

I was already too busy delving my tongue between her thighs to reply. I groaned instantly at the taste of her. It had been so long—how had I lasted so long without this?

Verity let out a strangled sound of pleasure, relaxing back onto the table and taking her weight off her arms. "That feels *so* good, Theon. Don't stop."

What a ludicrous idea. She'd told me to make her come until she couldn't walk. I had every intention of staying down here until I'd fulfilled her demands.

Power trickled through me in a slow, necessary stream. As much as I tried to stem it, not wanting to take anything from Verity, it had been weeks since I'd properly fed, and my body was acting in spite of my mind's instructions.

Verity came almost instantly with a breathy sigh, and I chastised myself for ignoring her physical needs. I was more than able to use my tongue on her while she rested comfortably on the bed.

I sat back on my heels, stroking the inside of Verity's thighs with my claws, giving her a moment of rest before I resumed my attentions.

"Kiss me," she demanded primly, struggling to sit up. I instantly stood, lifting her into a seated position on the table.

My tongue slid into her mouth, coated in her own essence, as I held back, always cautious of her slicing herself on my sharp teeth.

Verity smiled against my lips, wrapping her legs around my hips to urge me closer. "I need you too much. We can play a fun round of orgasm denial later when I'm not so fucking desperate for you."

The gratitude I felt at having such a mate was staggering in its intensity.

I dropped my shadows, tempering my strength as I dragged Verity to the edge of the table, grinding my cock into her soft wetness, coating myself in her slick.

Verity's arms wrapped around my shoulders, pulling me in close as I rocked my hips, my claws digging into her hips. I needed to get myself under control.

"Thank you, my love," I rambled, apologies and nonsense spilling from my lips. "You are too good to me. I'm so sorry I hurt you—"

"You're not in trouble for that," Verity panted, squirming impatiently against me. "You've apologized plenty for that."

"Thank you, thank you," I murmured. I hadn't even entered her yet and my knot was already beginning to swell, my vision turning hazy around the edges. "Tell me what else I did wrong, my love."

A fine sheen of sweat coated Verity's skin, her head tipped back toward the ceiling. "Were you even going to *try* get out of the Pit?"

I paused. That was what she was telling me off for?

"I deserved to be there, my love. I put your life in danger."

Verity swatted me on the shoulder before melting in my arms as I traced her mating mark with my tongue. "Next time we're separated, I fully expect you to move heaven and earth to get back to me, do you understand? I don't care if you're in prison or not. Make an effort."

"We will never be separated again," I promised her, carefully pulling the straps of her dress over her shoulders, my claws leaving faint pale lines on her skin.

"I'll hold you to that," she shot back, wriggling free enough to tug the dress down, her glorious breasts spilling over the top of the fabric, ripe for me to tease with my tongue. My beautiful, sensuous, fiery mate. I'd sooner cut off my horns than be parted from her again.

"I might die if I don't get your knot soon," Verity whined. "I've missed this so much."

"On your back," I ordered reflexively, already attempting to climb over her onto the table before pulling myself back, hearing the authority in my voice. It was natural to me. Far more natural than speaking calmly and considerately. But I needed to learn. I needed to give Verity soft, gentle, loving words.

"Well?" Verity asked, laying back and letting her legs drop open. "Are you going to fuck me into this table or not?

I breathed out, gentling my tone. "Of course, my love—"

Verity's foot pressed into my chest as I moved toward her, one eyebrow raised in disapproval. "Oh no. We are not doing that."

I stroked her extended leg softly. "Doing what?"

"Stop that. That thing you're doing. Do you not like the way we play?"

"Of course I like it. But after everything you've been through—"

"You better fuck me properly, *Your Grace*. You better pull my hair and wrap me in tentacles, and tell me I have a perfect greedy pussy. After you fuck my soul out of my body, then—and only then—you may resume being apologetic. But when we fuck, we *fuck*, you feel me? Because that's what we both enjoy."

My knot ached, desperate to be inside my mate.

"Are you sure, Verity? I don't want... I don't want you to think I don't care for you."

"You love me, and we both know it." She dropped her foot back to the table, letting me admire her pretty, weeping pussy. "*I* want this. I love your roughness, I love all of you. No one makes me come like you do," she added, all sultry desperation, knowing exactly how to manage me.

"Tell me if it's too much," I growled, climbing over her body and entering her in one smooth thrust and groaning at the feel of her hot, clasping cunt around me, as well as the rush of power that accompanied it.

"Power up, then give me those tentacles," Verity gasped, arching her back. "I want to feel you everywhere."

I gritted my teeth, pleasure already tingling at the base of my spine, threatening to overwhelm me. No, not until Verity had come again. Not until I'd given her the shadow fucking she was asking for.

Yes. I would be calm and restrained. I would draw this out, and give Verity the hours of pleasure she deserved.

"Oh, I should probably mention that my birth control shot has worn off," Verity added lightly. "If you come in me, there's a very good chance I'll end up pregnant."

I sucked in a breath, my knot expanding with my lungs. "Is that something you would want?"

"That's something I would want more than anything." Verity's smile was seductive and mischievous all at once, and any plans I'd had about making this last vanished from my brain.

The table creaked ominously beneath us as I started to move, my claws gouging deep lines into the wooden surface. If Verity conceived, I was going to have the table top mounted on the wall in our bedroom.

With a muffled shriek, Verity tightened around me and I pressed forward, lodging my knot into place as I filled her with my seed, trapping us together and hoping fervently that it would take. Just the idea of Verity round with my child had more cum spilling from my cock, a shiver of need running down my spine.

Whatever I had to do to make my mate and future children happy, I would do it. I would work side-by-side with my brothers. I would open every room of the manor for Verity's enjoyment. Hire more staff to restore the home to its former glory. Wait on my love hand and foot.

Whatever it was she asked of me, it would be my honor to provide.

"I love you," I murmured, gathering Verity up in my arms and rolling us so she could rest atop me. My purr immediately rumbled to life, the vibrations running through our bodies enhancing the feeling of being knotted together.

"I love you too," Verity replied dazedly, snuggling into my chest. "And I always will."

THEON

EPILOGUE

I can't believe you're working with the king," Rainy muttered, kicking a rock out of the way as she accompanied Verity and I back to Lindow after a morning at the palace. Verity had thought it would be good for Rainy to come along and see the cordial relationship I had established with Allerick and Damen, that it might soothe some of her discomfort about the changed situation.

It had been a very optimistic notion that had all the appearances of a spectacular failure, though I suspected it had gone a lot further in changing Rainy's opinion than she was letting on.

"You were not interested in the work we were doing?" I asked mildly, tucking Verity's arm further into the crook of mine.

"No," Rainy replied, far too quickly.

"My babies!" Mother cooed, throwing open the front doors of the manor, her arms outstretched as she waited for us to ascend the steps to the front porch. "Oh you've been gone for an *age*. I have been most discontent waiting for you to return!"

"You should have come with us," Verity laughed, slipping out of my grip with distressing ease to embrace my mother. "I'm sure Orabelle would have loved to see you."

My mother gave her a sly smile. "In truth, Orabelle finds me *very* grating. But so few people are willing to risk her wrath, I feel it is essential that I occasionally inflict my presence on her every now and again. It doesn't do one good to be sheltered from everyone and everything that inconveniences them."

Mother gave me an offensively pointed look at that.

"Is that why you're here?" I asked.

"Theon," Verity chided, swatting my arm affectionately. "He's kidding."

"I know," Mother assured her, beaming at us. "For my grumpy, reticent son has developed quite the sense of humor since you appeared in his life. And my daughter," she sighed, pulling a squirming Rainy into her embrace. "You've truly come into yourself in recent weeks."

"Get off, Mother," Rainy grumbled, though she wasn't trying very hard to get away, and she stopped wriggling while Mother cooed over the sparkling decorations Verity had stuck to my sister's claws.

"Wilder has prepared a special meal, if you're ready to eat now?" Mother asked, fussing with Rainy's hair.

"We'll meet you in the dining room," I said firmly, wrapping an arm around my mate's waist and guiding her through the foyer and upstairs.

Verity narrowed her eyes at me. "Don't get any ideas about having a quickie before lunch. I can't face your family smelling of sex pheromones again."

"I wouldn't dare," I murmured, suppressing a smile.

Rather than leading her to our third-floor bedroom, I headed for the "mistress dungeon," which had now been repurposed as a dressing room for Verity. Fester unfolded himself from a pile of cushions on the wide window ledge as we entered, and Verity crossed the candy-pink room to fuss over him.

"What are we doing here?" she asked absently, scratching between his ears while he rubbed his scent all over her. I would need to replace that later.

"I added something new to your jewelry box."

Verity gave me an indulgent look, the new caspite orb shining from the filigree cage that hung from her necklace, as well as a few other fine silver chains that I'd made her, layered over top.

"You don't need to keep making me things, you know. You've spoiled me enough as it is."

"My love, you don't believe those words for a second. You love when I give you gifts. You would be immensely disappointed if I ceased to."

Verity nodded solemnly. "You're right, I would. I was trying to seem less greedy."

I snorted, pulling the carved box off the shelf and presenting it to her. There was a strange, fluttering sort of feeling in my chest that I refused to concede was nerves.

Theon, Duke of Lindow, did not get nervous.

Verity's scent sweetened with excitement as she lifted the lid, before turning mellow and syrupy with the feeling I had come to associate with love.

"Is this...?" she breathed, carefully plucking the silver ring from the black velvet cushion. I had worked two thin bands of silver to twine around each other like vines, sculpting small leaves that fanned out either side. In the center, like a glowing bloom, was a pink sapphire Astrid had collected at my request, from the human realm.

"May I?" I murmured. Verity nodded, and I carefully took the ring between my claws, sliding it onto the ring finger of her left hand.

"Are you going to ask if I'll marry you?" Verity said breathlessly, her eyes glassy with tears, though her scent was still as sweet and intoxicating as ever.

"And risk you saying no? Absolutely not."

Verity laughed, one tear escaping as I slipped the ring onto her finger. She leaned forward, brushing a smiling kiss to my lips. "My answer is yes."

"Good. Then let us go downstairs, Wilder has been learning how to make your *pannekoek* to celebrate, and he believes he's finally got the recipe right—"

Verity was in my arms before I'd finished speaking, her legs wrapped around my hips, lips pressed to mine.

Verity was mine. My mate. My bride. And someday, the mother of my children. Being with Verity gave me more joy than I ever thought I would get to experience in my life, and I never intended on letting her go.

"What do you think?" Aderith asked, walking me through the temple that lay on the very outskirts of the estate. I'd spent the past few weeks out here myself, repairing the long-neglected building, though all of that hard work was currently hidden under dense floral arrangements. Mostly gray, though with the occasional hints of color that were now growing throughout the realm.

The pink flowers were at the front, on either side of the altar, all in order for this afternoon's ceremony.

"Who do we know that attended Allerick's wedding? I want to make sure we have more flowers than he did."

"I have already verified," Aderith said proudly, standing up a little taller. "The king made no effort for his own wedding. The temple was said to be quite dismal and uninviting."

"Excellent. Verity deserves the very best."

"As you say," Aderith agreed with a nod. "I will return to the kitchens if you are satisfied. I want to supervise these new staff, ensure that they don't make any mistakes on the most important day of your life."

I inclined my head in agreement, though her words weren't quite correct. The day I'd met Verity was the most important day of my life. This was just an opportunity to show the entire realm that she was mine and I was hers, if her bite didn't do enough to broadcast that already.

Satisfied that the temple was in order, I made my way back to the main house, which was bustling with staff—some brought on permanently, others hired for the occasion.

Verity had insisted that I not be allowed to see her before the ceremony, which seemed like an undue level of cruelty to inflict on her soon-to-be husband, but apparently, it was a human realm tradition she wished to maintain. Vastly dissatisfied with this, I slipped into one of the secret passages and made my way toward the sitting room where she was gathered with her friends, getting ready.

The mating bond led me directly there, and I took comfort in the fact that I wasn't *really* spying on her when she would sense my presence.

"He really bit you on the first night?" one of them was asking Verity. Tallulah, I thought, by the incredulous tone.

"Yup," Verity replied proudly. I found Tallulah's prim attitude trying, but Verity seemed to enjoy her company. Verity enjoyed *my* company though, which didn't speak well to her taste in companions. I would be forever grateful for it.

"That tracks," Tallulah replied faintly.

"What was your plan?" Austin laughed. "Just never tell anyone?"

"I'm sure it would have come up eventually," Verity said, the amusement clear in her voice. "Hold on one second, please."

I felt rather than heard her move, and suddenly her voice was much closer, as though she was speaking directly into the wall I was standing behind.

"Go away, darling."

"No," I grumbled, wishing I could see her face.

Verity laughed. "*Yes*. I'll see you soon, go spend some time with your brothers. Have some food. Be a good host."

"We always have our midday meal together."

I heard the smile in her voice. "We're going to eat soon. Go find your brothers and we can at least be having our midday meal at the same time. And from tomorrow, we'll never miss one again. Deal?"

There was a chorus of *awwws* behind her that did a better job at sending me running than her encouraging words did.

"I'll see you at the end of the aisle, okay?" Verity asked softly.

"You can be sure of it. Until then, my love."

THANK YOU

What a ride. This book—or rather, Theon, in particular—was inspired by the Phantom of the Opera, who really picked up where the Beast from Beauty and the Beast left off in my toxic-trait awakening. I hope you enjoyed his over-the-top, dramatic energy, I certainly enjoyed writing him! And let's not forget Verity. After Selene and Astrid, I was keen to write a very different kind of FMC. Verity is no warrior, but she absolutely has her own kind of quiet strength and badassery, and it was a total joy to explore.

I need to say a few quick thank yous—starting with you, reader <3 I couldn't do this without you, so thank you so much for taking a chance on this series. I'd also like to say an extra special thank you to my Ream subscribers, I'm so grateful for your support.

A special thanks to Dr T, my real-life doctor friend who answered all my brain injury questions with quiet bemusement, and the occasional... "isn't this book about monster sex?"

Thank you to the wonderful Steph at Rawls Reads Editing and Marcelle at Books Checked—absolute editing rockstars as always. Thank you Rory for beta reading, I love you <3 I also have to thank my PA, Nikki, and all of my friends, for encouraging me to actually stay on task and write this thing. I love you guys.

Colette R. xx

P.S. To keep up with the latest news and releases, join my Facebook Reader Group or subscribe to my newsletter.

ABOUT THE AUTHOR

Colette Rhodes is a paranormal romance author from New Zealand. She loves to write about love in all its forms, and adores imperfect heroes and heroines who find perfection in each other. You'll often find her trying to justify her degree by including ancient history and mythological influences in her work.

If she's not writing, then you're almost certain to find her reading—ideally with a cup of tea in hand and a scented candle burning to match the mood.

Keep up with Colette here:
coletterhodes.com
@coletterhodes_author

ALSO BY COLETTE

SHADES OF SIN:

Luxuria

Superbia

Gula

Avaritia

Invidia

Ira

Acedia

STATE OF GRACE:

Run Riot

Silver Bullet

Wild Game

Dare Not

Saving Grace

THREE BEARS DUET:

Gilded Mess

Golden Chaos

LITTLE RED DUET:

Scarlet Disaster

Seeing Red

KNOTTY BY NATURE:

(RH omegaverse with T.S. Snow)

Allure Part 1

Allure Part 2

EMPATH FOUND:

The Terrible Gift

The Unwanted Challenge

The Reluctant Keeper

DEADLY DRAGONS:

The (Not) Cursed Dragon

The (Not) Satisfied Dragon

STANDALONE:

Dead of Spring (MF - Hades & Persephone retelling)

Scheme (MF omegaverse)